LADY STARDUST

Edited by Art Critic Panda

Obverse Books
info@obversebooks.co.uk
www.obversebooks.co.uk
Cover Design by Paul Hanley
First published September 2012

Introduction © Art Critic Panda
Slip Away © Scott Liddell
Hang Onto Yourself © Paul Magrs
Low/Profile © George Mann
Modern Love © Alan Taylor
Up the Hill Backwards © Nick Campbell
Cracked Actor ©Stewart Sheargold

Iris and Panda © Paul Magrs

Thanks to Jeremy Hoad and David Bowie

Printed and bound in Great Britain by inkylittlefingers

Contents

Letter from the Editor

Dear Readers,

Panda here. I was asked to scribble a few words by way of introduction to this stupendous tome. So here I am, G&T at my side, a bit of Cilla on the stereogram, and pen in hand.

First, I must say what a marvellous pleasure it has been to edit such a beautifully written collection of stories about me and that Iris woman. Usually I try to keep a low profile in our adventures but really, when one is knocking around with that floozy it is rather tricky. I do love the woman dearly but sometimes I just have to slip away for a bit of quiet panda time to recover. Just the other day we had to retreat at speed from some horror or other back up the hill to the bus. And bloody backwards. I ask you, no thought for a small panda with short legs and not too good balance at the best of times. I mean, up the hill backwards at my age. No respect. She can be a selfish cow sometimes. A spot of splashy splashy, though, and I was ready to set off again.

You might notice I am nude on the cover. Well, last week I had a lovely afternoon resting in the Jardin du Luxembourg and just popped into Le Bon Marché on my way back to the bus for a spot of browsing and saw the most marvellous, stripey cravat after a little detour in La Grande Epicerie. Blue, green and purple it was with a lovely gold trim (the cravat, not the épicerie). On my return to the bus I managed to wake herself from her afternoon stupor all I got was 'Oh, hello Panda dear. New cravat? How very modern, love'. Typical. We had a terrible row and I threw my new cravat behind the chaise lounge in disgust. Iris accused me of overreacting and behaving like a precious actor after a bad review. I tossed an empty bottle of Bombay Sapphire at her so hard when it bounced off the window it cracked. 'Actor, indeed, you're one to talk' I mused. 'Hang onto yourself, Panda, it's going to be one of

5

those evenings'. Iris only managed to calm me down after a few cocktails and a promise of dinner at Le Meurice. Then the photographer arrived. Hence the nudey panda cover. I don't think people will notice, though, what with Iris doing one of her impressions of Worzel Gummidge's sister.

Anyway, I hope you enjoy this collection. I went through a whole box of red pencils editing the fucking thing and still haven't received my case of gin in recompense yet. Bloody publishers. Shower of amateurs.

Panda (Editor)

Modern Love

Alan Taylor

Etherweb Chat Client v2.36a Enabled.
Connecting... connecting
Connected at 03:27:22. Go.

Hi Rainbow. It's me, Felix – sorry I'm late. <<<<Hugs>>>> Glad you're still awake, though – and really sorry if you were worried about me. I took a detour on the way back to my apartment, you see – supposed to be a short cut, it was. Ha.

It could only have happened to me, though. Because I'm post-human. I know we don't talk about that much, but it's an important part of who I am, and an important part of what happened to me tonight. So I'm mentioning it now so it's in your head when I tell you everything that happened.

Anyway, back to my story. The beginning bit. You know I've told you about the lane behind the clinics at the hospital – between them and the short term wards? Remember, the one I avoid because it doesn't smell right? It smells like a wet Tuesday, no matter what day it is.

Well, I decided that if I got off my shift right on time, at 5.15, before the sun shaded down to greasy twilight, I would be big enough and brave enough to walk down it. Now that the nights are getting shorter I love the burnt orange sky as the sun sets over the mountains on the colony's Western border. I figured it'd shave a good five minutes off my walk to the subway station. It probably would have done, but as I passed the back of Emergency Genetic Remanipulation Ward 10 I noticed this large rectangular shadow.

Now I know I should have pulled back, cowered away, I know it, but something about me made me look closer. It was only a bus, wasn't it? An old Earth bus – one of the ones where you can jump on at the back. Number 22.

Well, you know me. I try to be minimal, efficient. I know when to go out. I know when to stay in. I get things done. But I like investigating, I like helping people, and one of these days my curiosity is going to kill me. So I did what was probably the most stupid thing to do with a strange bus like that. I went inside.

I've not been on a bus before – dare say you haven't either – but between you and me I always thought they'd be kind of like the monorails on most of the fringe colonies. You know – seats. For people to sit on. I didn't expect a candelabra. I didn't expect curtains with flowers on them. I didn't expect a table and chairs, a teapot, a half eaten sandwich. I didn't expect a woman of a certain age lying on a bed of fur coats.

We've discussed before how I'm not good with descriptions of people. I try hard, but most human beings look pretty much the same to me. I can tell one gender from another, most of the time, and this person was definitely a woman, but apart from that? She looked kind of ordinary. Frail, though. Pale skin, almost transparent, like her body was wearing thin. She had a dignity to her. I could see her being quite imposing if she wanted to be. A wide mouth that I could imagine smiling. She was dressed in a dark green tweed jacket and matching skirt, a pearl necklace, and an oversized hat – and her hands were clasped in front of her. She'd clearly been placed there, arranged that way. There was something more about her, though. She didn't smell quite human, but that's not uncommon on Algeria Touchshriek. She looked like she was dead, but she didn't have that lingering scent that the dead do. So I checked her pulse. It was faint, and it was so, so slow. But it was there.

'She's alive.' I don't know why I said it aloud, but I did.

'What do you mean she's alive?'

Took me a second to work out who had said that, didn't it? And you know what? It was only her teddy bear – her stuffed panda. It – he – had been sitting in a dark corner of the bus, watching me all the time I'd been on board the bus. Watching. Kind of creepy, when you think about it.

'I said what do you mean she's alive?' His voice: angry, concerned and relieved in roughly equal measure.

'You're a stuffed Panda.'

'And you're a six foot tall talking cat. Don't get so bloody personal.'

Now I know what you're thinking, and I thought it too. But I figured he must be some sort of android or something. Pandroid? Is that even a word? It doesn't really matter what he was – he was there, he was talking to me, and that meant that he was – whatever that was. People look funny at me, the first time they see me. But if they get talking to me, they get over it. Same with Panda.

Yes, the Panda's name was Panda. We discussed it on the way to the lab, later on – I'll get on to that bit in a bit, but I think I laughed when he told me his name. To which his response was 'Felix the Cat? Really?'

Anyway, back to the bus, and the woman, and Panda being concerned.

'She's not breathing, but she's got a pulse. Very slow, but it's there.' I had no way of knowing what was going on in her brain, but I didn't tell Panda that. 'In short, she's alive. But comatose.'

'Oh Iris,' sighed Panda. He turned to the woman – 'You said you could bypass your respiratory system, and I just assumed you were making it up as usual, you silly old woman' – and then back to me – 'so how do we snap her out of it?'

I took a deep breath. 'That depends.'

Thing is, Rainbow, I've not been a doctor for that long, and most of that time's been dealing with scraped knees and infectious diseases of the rich and insured. Comas were something I'd only read about – but I know enough to know that the key to understanding a coma is knowing what was going on leading up to it. I told Panda as much and he told me what he and Iris had been through.

They had just escaped, it seemed, from an aberrant universe where there was no such thing as alcohol. After about ten minutes of moaning, Iris had adapted and learned to cope without it. They had met a shape changing penguin killer monk and together the three of them had endured many adventures that Panda described as 'interminably boring'. Eventually, it had turned out that the entire aberrant universe had been actually a single planet that had been locked in a space box or something, and had been redecorated between their adventures. Citing boredom, Iris and Panda had escaped back to our universe through a trap door under a pile of books in the corner of a library made out of kittens.

'I know,' said Panda when I looked puzzled. 'It made precious little sense to me, and I was there. We got back on the bus, ran over the monk, crashed back in to the real universe, and then Iris looked at me and said 'gin', and collapsed. And I've been here ever since. It's been three days now. I'm getting bored.'

'So have you given her some gin?'

'I thought she was dead. I don't know about you, but I'm not in the habit of pouring good liquor down the throats of corpses. It's perverse. Anyway, we don't have any. Iris drank it all as soon as we got to the aberrant universe. Have you got any?'

I shook my head, and explained about Algeria Touchshriek being a medical outpost, and alcohol being prohibited except for research purposes. I went in to some detail about the colony seeding programme here in the outer worlds, about the city-ships landing and unfolding in to single purpose flat pack settlements, but Panda started yawning very obviously, so I stopped talking.

After a long pause, he said 'So. No. Alcohol. At all.'

'No,' I replied.

Panda seemed quite... put out by this, and I learned a few new expletives that I'm too ashamed to type to you. He was quite enthusiastic about it, and most of the universe appeared to be the target of his wrath.

And then he broke off mid-insult. I think he had described me as a freakish half breed and the entire idea of a medical colony world as an economically unsustainable whimsy, when he stopped, looked at me and said 'Research labs.'

'What?'

'That's where we'll find some alcohol. For research. And probably recreation, too, if I know medical researchers. They'll be sipping the medicinal brandy to cope with the dreary tedium of medical research.'

So we went to the research labs. I offered to go on my own, but Panda insisted on coming too. Something about not trusting me to come back. Abandonment issues, for sure. I carried him, tucked inside my jacket, and took the quick route, over the rooftops.

Why did I do it? Good question, Rainbow, good question. Why didn't I just tell Panda where to go and come home to chat to you? It's the medic in me, I think. Iris needed my help – medical help – and I couldn't abandon her. But more than that, I was nosey. I'd been in the research centre compound a few times, and I'd seen the labs but I'd never been inside. I wondered what went on in there – I was curious. Helping Panda and Iris – that was just the excuse I'd been looking for.

Anyway, I know you like to keep track of these things, so you'll be glad to know that this was when we introduced ourselves formally, but we didn't talk too much, mainly because I was running, and Panda was tucked inside my jacket.

The research centre's near the geriatric wards, and it's basically a whole bunch of warehouses that are used as a mixture of storage and laboratories. It's walled, with only one point of access, but once you're inside, there's nothing much in the way of security, just a few cameras. From the outside, it looks secure, but you can get in to the grounds if you're nimble, and you've got no problems leaping up a five metre wall. Easy enough for me. Panda wasn't happy though. I spotted the cameras, timed my leap carefully and landed on all fours just inside the compound rolling forward into a blind spot in the security sweep.

'That,' he said, 'is not a dignified way to travel.'

'I did offer to come alone,' I reminded him.

'And I'm beginning to wish I'd let you.'

I crouched in the shadow of a suspended walkway, watching the slow movements of the cameras, measuring their rhythm.

'If we're quick we can get in and out quickly. You can get back to Iris and I can get home to Rainbow.'

'Rainbow? What sort of a name is Rainbow?'

I bared my teeth at Panda, just to let him know I was annoyed by his question. I told him that Rainbow was the name that you'd chosen for yourself. I think it's a beautiful name. I think it suits you.

'So,' said Panda after a brief pause. 'Pretty, is she? Your girlfriend?'

'I don't know. I've never seen her.'

'Never seen her? Do it in the dark, do you? Hardly the basis of a healthy relationship.'

'I mean we've never met. Not physically. We chat on the etherweb, though. We talk every day, and we talk about everything. It means we really get to know each other – our true selves, without being worried about appearances.'

'Seems pretty silly to me. And Rainbow's still a stupid name.'

'I still like it.'

'I wouldn't go telling people that. They'll think you're an imbecile.'

The red light on the top of the nearest camera went out and the slow pan to its new position began. I took the opportunity to run for the nearest door – on all fours for speed. This had the lucky side effect of shutting Panda up.

The main research lab. I'd not been in it since the induction course. It reminded me of the lab that I grew up in, back on TVC15. Converted from a colony ship's cargo hold. Concrete floor, steel walls, and shipping containers stacked up inside to give some sort of structure to the cavernous space. Fluorescent strip lighting. And huge. I had forgotten how huge these places were.

'This place is enormous,' said Panda, pulling out of my grasp.

'So we should start looking,' I said. I flashed him my smile that shows how sharp my teeth are and manages to be both friendly and threatening.

'Well, yes.'

They say that humans have five senses, but I'm only partly human, and I've got many more. I don't have names for them all, so I call a lot of them smell. There's not a better word for them. And something about the way that the far corner of the laboratory was laid out drew me there. It looked like the holding pens on TVC15, where they would put us when we misbehaved – me and the other genetic freaks that they were experimenting with. Back before it all closed down.

I don't think I've said much about TVC15 before, have I? One of the Phase Two worlds, where the law was generally felt to be optional. I grew up there. I was born there. In a lab. I was made by scientists using grafted and spliced human and cat DNA. Little bits of left over genetic material that nobody else wanted. And I was not alone.

The scientists that made us said we were the first post-humans. They said that we were beautiful, they said that we were special. They valued us, but only in the sense that I value my job. We were something for them to do. They didn't love us, though sometimes they said that they did. They thought of us as things that they had made, nothing more. I hated the cold hearted cynicism, I hated imprisonment, and I hated them. I was never more happy than the day I was when we were liberated, and I was granted my freedom as a full citizen of the colony worlds. Even then, I never saw the sky on TVC15.

The area at the far corner of the lab smelled like the lab where I grew up. I was drawn to it, couldn't keep away from it.

Panda, meanwhile, had found a likely looking cupboard and was attacking the padlock with a chair leg.

I turned a corner of a wall of shipping containers and came to a sudden halt.

They're doing the same thing on Algeria Touchshriek that they were doing on TVC15.

Two rows of containers, glass walled, facing each other. Stacked four high, and stretching from where I stood at one end of the hangar to the giant double doors at the other. Candidate cells, they were called. Individual survival chambers, soundproofed and climate controlled. And in each, a single person. Some sleeping, some tapping away at etherweb terminals, but most just sitting there, looking out. I knew that haunted look, that feeling of hopelessness. Most of them looked like they were post-human. Some were cat people, like myself. There were a few dog-men, at least one Rhinoceroid, and many more where the genetic synthesis was in a state of decay. There were even some that looked perfectly human. I wondered what their story was.

I knew the technology. I recognised it. I grew up inside it, watching people use it, people who thought that they were better than me. Half way down the corridor I spotted the control desk, midway between both walls of Candidate cells. I knew how the controls worked. These people were the closest thing I had to family. I had to set them free.

'There you are!'

Panda ran up to me as fast as he could, looking like he was out of breath, although I doubted that was physically possible. In his paws he was clutching a half bottle of Gin. And that was pretty much when the trap was sprung.

I don't know if there was any warning, but I was distracted by Panda anyway. I must have triggered some sort of sensor, I guess, or a laser trip wire. Or maybe they had been scanning my DNA since I broke in to the lab, checking my records, seeing if I was a suitable fit. It doesn't matter. One moment I was grinning at Panda in triumph, and the next I was in a force cage; I was encaged in a cone of laser beams shot from an emitter in the ceiling. Fine lines of red light, crisscrossing into a cone around me – easily three metres wide at the base, and the point so high in the roof I couldn't make it out. I felt the slight warmth of the cage, smelled the burning of dust particles where they danced through the fine burning lines in the air. Trapped.

Panda summed up our position best. 'Bollocks,' he said.

A low pitched hum started on the control desk. I knew the standard incursion procedure from TVC15. Electrify the controls, and probably an area of floor too. I knew what was coming next too. A recorded message.

'Welcome, specimen 392. You have been identified as a subject of genetic interest, and have therefore been restrained under section 28, sub-clause 8 of the Algeria Touchshriek colony regulations pertaining to civil liberties and suspension thereof. Please do not attempt to leave the force cage as to do so will almost certainly damage you unnecessarily. Please make yourself as comfortable as you can. An alarm has been sounded and someone will catalogue you within eight hours. Thank you for your patience.'

'Thank you for your patience? Thank you for your patience?' Panda was incensed. Again.

'This is how it always happens, you know. Every time! She goes and gets herself in to some sort of bother, and I end up having to bail her out of it. And that ends me up in even more trouble. And is she ever grateful? Is she? I almost died in the ice caves of Canthrop Minor when she was munching on chocolate footballs at the ambassador's reception. I could have died of toxaemia once, while she was busy being turned in to a giant canary. And now, stuck in a dingy cell with you, while she's having a big nap. A big nap, I ask you? The ignominy. I'm going to die here, you know. They'll come for me, well, they'll come for us, but when they see me they'll want to cut me open, see how I work. There'll be innards everywhere, I tell you. A real, well, mess. So to speak.'

'Have you finished?' I asked, wondering what Panda's innards might look like.

'Yes.' He sat down, head on his paws, sulking.

I gave him a minute before I asked him.

'You didn't die in the ice caves, though, did you? Or of toxaemia?'

15

'I could have done though. If Iris hadn't persuaded the Siberian Controller to knock down the ice caves and buy a giant thermos flask I'd still be there now. And she did swap her signed photograph of Fanny Craddock for the cure for the toxaemia, I suppose.'

'Well, she needs you now Panda. You're small enough to get between the bars of the energy cage. You should go to her.'

'She's the most annoying, self-obsessed, frustrating woman in the universe.'

'She's your friend. You love her. I get it.'

'Love her?' Panda cleared his throat, almost violently. 'I don't know about that. I tolerate her, yes. And I look after her. Someone has to. She gets herself in to the most terrible scrapes, you know.'

'So you should go to her. Take her the gin. Wake up Sleeping Beauty and go off on your adventures in time and space.'

For a second, I thought Panda was going to protest, and offer to stay with me. But I'd have made him leave, and I think he knew that. He left, clutching the gin close to his furry chest. I think it was the right thing to do. He did look over his shoulder at me before he left, a look of regret on his tiny furry face.

I was so jealous of Iris then.

Not that I knew her, of course. I couldn't even be sure I'd remember her face if I saw her again, though she did have that unique smell. But Iris had Panda. A true friend, someone who loved her, who looked out for her. Even if he was irritating.

In all my life, I've had nobody like that. Growing up in the lab I didn't even really have friends. Some of the technicians and lab assistants were okay, but they didn't look at me like a person. They looked at me like an experiment, or a pet. Some of them wouldn't talk to me. They'd talk about me instead, like I wasn't there in front of them.

The other post-humans in the lab weren't much better. We were allies rather than friends. They kept us separate most of the time, but occasionally they'd see how we interact, and we'd talk. But we'd talk about escape, and rebellion – we wouldn't talk about feelings. We wouldn't talk about who we were.

Then I was liberated, did my medical studies on Optimus Prime, and I met people. Real people. I didn't know how to react to them, I guess. I'd walk through the campus on my own, and I'd think that everyone was looking at me. I was even suspicious of the people who wanted to be my friends. I was the scary cat person. The one with all the attitude. How cool would it be to be my friend? I could have been wrong. I probably was. But it was what I knew, that shield.

And now, now I have you. And you're special, Rainbow, really you are. You're the only person I talk to, ever, really. And I tell you everything, and you remember and you listen and you ask me questions and you're brilliant, really you are. Remember how nervous I was when I first told you I was a cat. I was really scared you'd reject me. But you didn't. We started off without preconceptions, which is great. But I don't know you, Rainbow. I don't know your real name, I don't know where you are. I don't even know if the photo you sent was real. You could be anyone. You could be a different person every time I chat to you. Hell, you could even be a machine.

I'm sorry, Rainbow. That was mean. That was unfair. I do think you're real, really I do. But when I was sitting on the floor in the force cage, I was thinking terrible things like that. I was angry at everything, but mainly angry at myself. I thought I'd never be able to tell you how much you mean to me. I know you have a good heart, Rainbow. I know your soul. I know I love you.

When I realised that, when I admitted that to myself, that's when I knew I had to work out a way to get out of there. I had you to come back to. Even if it was just to get back to this dorm room, to this terminal to log in and tell you I'm okay. I figured they'd send a scientist to get me, probably just one, unarmed except for a tranq gun. They'd turn off the force cell from the central control panel, and I'd have maybe a second to either jump them or escape. It wasn't really enough, but it was worth a shot. I settled down for a nap, figuring I'd hear them coming. A cat nap, if you must.

17

I didn't have long to wait before I heard something. It was a little more than footsteps though. The big double doors at the end of the lab burst open which was a little unexpected, although I should have expected it. The bus. The number 22 bus. Iris driving it, awake now, and full of life and, doubtless, gin. As it barrelled down the wide corridor I could have sworn I heard a cry of 'Woo hoo lovey', and then a whoop of delight as Iris threw the bus into a spin, skidding to a halt, ploughing through the control desk, sending chunks of it flying in various directions, including a large piece that headed straight for me and burned up on the laser cage, just as the cage itself deactivated. And there, at the back of the bus, Panda. Waving.

I think I can honestly say I've never been happier to see a stuffed animal in my life.

'You know what?' he said, in that gruff voice of his. 'Sometimes I believe in second chances. I'm that sort of Panda.'

Iris was... well, she was exuberant. She clambered down from the driver's cab of the bus and threw her arms around me like a long-lost friend. 'So you're Felix,' she said. 'Panda didn't mention you were so good looking.'

I didn't know where to look when she said that. I was suddenly very aware that I could use a shower. I imagine I blushed. Iris laughed at me. She had the laugh of a much younger woman.

She insisted that I joined her in a large gin, to thank me. We drank it out of china cups, sitting on the back step of the bus. I can't say I liked it much. She didn't bat an eyelid when I poured the last of it in to my saucer to make it easier to drink, though. I purred, acknowledging her discretion.

'No need to be self-conscious around me and Panda, lovey. We've seen some strange things in our times. I've seen stranger things before breakfast. Done stranger too, no doubt. Did Panda tell you about the time when I wrestled Queen Victoria for the right to rule Ursa Minor in a non-regulation singlet? That was a strange day, let me tell you.'

Iris looked around the cages, then. Some of the post-humans looked back at Iris.

'Looks like we've got some work to do here, Panda,' she said. This was clearly something she was looking forward to.

'Are you pondering what I'm pondering?' asked Panda.

'A little bit of constructive vandalism? That's what I do best.'

I believed her. I offered to help – I wanted to help. For the first time in years, I felt *alive*, Rainbow. I felt like these people needed me, and I could make a difference. Maybe it was the gin. But Iris was having none of it. She said that she and Panda were experienced professionals – a statement that I only half believed – and then she told me I should come back home so I could tell you I was all right. I don't want you to worry about me, Rainbow, really I don't. Not ever.

Iris said something to me then, something I thought I'd share with you. She said that the universe is a big place, and parts of it are very boring, and parts of it are very strange. She said that there are worlds out there where the trees are asleep, where bus stations fly from village to village, where the skies are pink and the moons age and daydream. Somewhere there's injustice. Somewhere there's danger. But everywhere you go, people love each other. Every love is different; some love is passionate, some is irrational, some is unrequited and most is downright silly. Some is so insane that it starts wars, while some is so intimate that it's almost invisible. But it's everywhere.

Love, she said, is all around us. And then Panda threw a teacup at her.

Anyway, that's why I'm late. And that's why I'm going back to help. To help Iris, and tohelp all those poor caged post-humans work out what they want to do with their freedom. Because I think that's what I can do best. And there's something else. I think I'm ready now.

I'd like to meet you, my love.

What do you say?

Waiting... waiting...

19

Hang onto Yourself

Paul Magrs

1979. On the Planet Previously known as Glam.

It really was called that, once upon a time. Mr Glister could hardly credit it. What a shame they had changed it. The new designation – now that the planet was about to join the Loose Alliance – was the far more prosaic M-21b. Vince had been right, thought the sad dwarf. Everything in the modern day universe was tending towards the dour and glum. The Seventies were ending and everyone was feeling a little sadder and wiser.

Vince himself had wandered out into the wilderness, here on this alien world. His diminutive chum hadn't seen him for several days. It had been Monday when Vince suddenly appeared in a thin, white cotton shift, looking all monkish and solemn. He declared that he was walking out into the crimson desert to make his tribute to the great gods of Glam. He didn't want any provisions or any company on his pilgrimage. His face was devoid of make-up and glitter. His hair was back in its natural shade of dirty brown.

He really has changed, thought Glister. He really means it this time. He is retiring for good. He is striding out into the inhospitable wastes of Glam and renouncing his calling forever.

That morning Mr Glister had shed a tear or two for the passing of the rock star known as Vince Cosmos.

'It's all right, Mr Glister, old pal,' Vince had said, grimly. 'I'll still be the same person. I just won't be quite the same on the outside. We can have some peace at last, eh?'

But, thought Mr Glister, as he watched his friend shimmer on the horizon and eventually disappear like a wavering mirage... But I liked all the fuss and the kerfuffle of the rock star world. I loved the screaming crowds and the autographs, the tour buses and the concert appearances. I liked humping the equipment about and acting as his security guard. Even the boring stuff, like hanging around the studios as he worked so painstakingly on his lyrics – even all that was thrilling. And also... I liked our secret mission too. The stuff that our public never knew we were up to. Our endless, dangerous task of saving the world from the Visitors...

He went to sit in the courtyard of the old stone house. He sipped mint tea and smoked something that had been left lying around on the tiled table, which made him see double for a while. He wasn't even sure who this house belonged to. Typical of Vince – to dump him here and go off seeking his own spiritual salvation or whatever he was up to. Glister was feeling a bit annoyed, actually. Parsecs from home and unable to even speak the language.

Here came that older woman again, in the midnight blue robes. She was so graceful and kind-looking. She had kissed and hugged Vince. Glister had wondered whether they were related. Maybe this was Vince's mother or aunty. She smiled and nodded at the dwarf and brought him sticky sweetmeats on golden dishes. Oh, what am I anyway? thought Glister miserably. Just a helper. Nothing more than a Roadie, really. Why should I have anything explained to me, anyway?

He fell into a vexed daydream of those early days with Vince. Back before the boy was mega-famous. When they lived on the houseboat in Camden and Vince was a rising star, appearing on BBC TV's *Smashing Tunes* and at the Royal Variety Performance. When Poppy Munday first joined their gang as Vince's P.A and they had had to explain to her about the Martians infiltrating Earth show-business and how they were the spearhead of another Martian invasion force. That plucky Geordie girl had taken the whole thing in her stride... What a team they had made!

Seven years later, though, their little gang was broken. After all those years of hits and shows and fights with Martians. Now they were split up. The band had gone its separate ways. Poppy was in New York. Vince and Glister were here... somewhere down in space. The scarlet

21

and lilac, mountainous world that Vince claimed to come from. True, he had grown up in East Dulwich, but this was his true home, he had earnestly explained. This was where his roots were. The planet once known as Glam.

Days and days had gone by and there was no sign of Vince. Glister was left to his own devices. He wasted time checking over and polishing the instruments and dials of their small spacecraft. He sighed as he gazed at all that polished brass and wood, knowing that he only really understood half of the principles that guided their spaceship's flight from Earth. If the worst was to happen and Vince never returned from his arid vigil, then Glister wouldn't stand a chance of returning home. At this, he shuddered with repressed panic.

The woman Glister suspected of being related to Vince came by to see him that evening as the servants brought him more of their rich, somewhat sticky dishes. She made consoling crooning noises and he nodded crossly at her. If she really was Vince's mother, did she understand much about her son, and the life he had lived on Earth in the Seventies? Did she even understand what a Glam Rock star was? Had she ever heard the marvelous tracks that Vince had cut?

Up here, in these calm, lofty realms, all that hullabaloo seemed almost irrelevant. Something bridled inside Mr Glister at that thought. He felt as if Vince was casting off everything that had ever connected them. Everything they had striven to achieve. Like the planet itself, Vince Cosmos had renounced his glitter.

When darkness fell that night Mr Glister made a snap decision and stole a small landcraft that was docked outside the main gates of the complex. It seemed easy enough to drive. After a few false starts he got it hovering across the desert sands. No one shouted out and came running to stop him. His heart leapt up at the sudden jolt of speed as he flew full throttle into the cooling sands.

How would he even know where Vince had gone? This whole world was covered in red sand. He could lose himself in it and never get back to civilization. Just at that moment, though, Glister didn't care. He flew blindly into the moonlit night and trusted that he would find his friend and employer by sheer instinct.

He knew Vince was going to the mountains. He had heard him mention that he intended to perform the self-purifying ritual of Pann'baaa at the Mountain of Quo. As he rode along, Glister activated the car's small computer screen and plugged in a query. The route to the Mountain of Quo twinkled into being. The car adjusted its direction and he sighed contentedly. He would be there in just under three hours.

Glister sat back, watching the swooping dark clouds perform a dance just for him under the golden moonlight. He found he was whispering a song or two by Vince as he anticipated a reunion with his chum.

But when he came to the mountain he was surprised to be flagged down by a very small person, standing alone in the road. A person even smaller than Mr Glister.

Glister slowed down. There was a Panda waving at him. He blinked. A toy Panda: not even a real one. And now the Panda was dashing up to the side of the space age car Glister had purloined. Oh, this was too much.

'Hallo, Mr Glister,' the small bear said.

The dwarf stared at him. 'You know me?'

'You need to come with me,' said Panda, straightening out his cravat, which had become ruffled in the breeze. 'There's someone who wants to talk to you.'

'Got no time,' said Glister grimly. 'I'm looking for my friend.'

'Yes, we know that,' sighed Panda. 'We've been keeping tabs on you both.'

'You know where Vince is?'

But the Panda was evasive, suddenly. He hopped into the driver's cab next to the dwarf and patted the dashboard commandingly. Then he started giving directions, which took them and their stolen hovercar into the dusky foothills of the Mountains of Quo. And there, standing proudly on a gentle mound, was a double decker bus.

'The Number 22 to Putney Common,' gasped Mr Glister. 'I used to catch that when I was working on the building sites...'

'Not this one,' Panda laughed.

Next thing, they were letting themselves aboard the bus, and Glister had time enough to notice that all the windows were obscured by chintz curtains. The hydraulic doors whooshed open and suddenly he and the small bear were standing inside what seemed to be a really messy boudoir. There was a chaise longue and an Art Deco cocktail cabinet and various other pieces of antique furniture. Items of fancy clothing and star charts were slung any old how about the place.

'You hoo?' Panda called.

Mr Glister fought to keep control of himself. Here he was, on a bus on this alien world. In the company of a toy someone might have won at the fair. And yet he had faced much stranger things in the past.

Panda dashed up the stairwell to the top deck. Glister heard him talking to someone. A female voice. Slightly slurred. Less than a minute later there was a slimmish blonde with purple highlights crashing down those metal stairs. She wore a tiger print frock coat and yellow plastic stack heel boots and she'd stuck golden stars on her face – just for him.

'Mr Glister,' she cried, sticking a tremulous hand in his face for him to kiss. 'How lovely. I do like a nice little man.'

He scowled at her. 'Who the hell are you?'

Her face fell. 'Don't you know me? Oh dear. Iris Wildthyme, Mr Glister. Transtemporal adventuress.'

Glister accepted a Martini and sat on the cluttered chaise longue, balancing the silvery glass in both hands. The Wildthyme woman was regaling him with all sorts of tales about how she and her Panda friend came to be on the planet formerly known as Glam. For a few minutes

Glister was happy to sip his murderously strong drink – after having lived off mint tea since he had touched down on Glam with Vince a week ago.

He stared fretfully at the chattering baglady as she said, 'What I'm interested in is why Vince is retiring now. Why's he giving up the ghost?'

'He feels like he's old hat,' said Glister. 'There's no secret about that. His records don't sell in anything like their old numbers. Even he could see that Glam is dead. He kept on going though – through the soul revival, and Disco... and then punk and now New Wave on its way. He kept on churning out his records. He even tried his hand at a disco number.'

'Heard it,' Panda growled. 'It was diabolical.'

'Oh, I rather liked it,' grinned Iris. 'But it's rather more, isn't it, Mr Glister, than simply retiring from the music biz? Vince is giving up his other role, too, isn't he? His more secretive and hush-hush role as defender of the Earth?'

Glister boggled at her. 'How do you know about that?'

She batted her fake eyelashes at him and he saw that they were clogged with black and silver glitter. 'One has one's methods, dear,' she said.

Glister stared at her levelly. 'You know... I've had a feeling... ever since I stepped aboard this bus of yours... We've met before, haven't we?'

'I couldn't possibly say,' she smiled. 'Now look, Mr Glister. If your boss has renounced his Glam ways and his Rock 'n' Roll lifestyle, that's all very well. But he can't just leave the Earth undefended against the alien Visitors.'

'Indeed not,' said Panda hotly.

'We need his map,' Iris said, leaning forward, and breathing ginny fumes into Glister's face. 'The special map, remember?'

The special map... he wondered. And he wondered hard, and he wondered some more. Glister knew that he'd shot his memory to merry hell throughout the Seventies with substance abuse and standing near the speakers at too many gigs. He had shaken the sense out of himself, was what Poppy Munday always used to say...

That was a point... where had Poppy Munday gone? When had she gone? New York, wasn't it? She was working in the New York office near Times Square... it was okay, he could remember. And the last time they saw her was when Vince took that suite and there was the aftershow party and Jimmy Bellotron had turned up with Fiji and all their gang...

Glister sat watching the Maelstrom stream by outside the bus, and consoled himself with the thought that – yes – if he tried hard enough, he could, in fact, remember things. He dreaded the coming 1980s, though – imagining further decline in all his faculties.

Iris was in the cab of the bus, and she had taken them off into this swimmy, orange and greenish hyperspatial dimension where 'space and time are completely buggered up', as Panda had put it. Now they were at least a trillion light years from Vince and his Zennish sojourn in the Mountains of Quo and this made Glister feel very uneasy. But there was nothing he could do, could he? This was tantamount to kidnap by this old ratbag and her bear. He lay back on the chaise longue, pulling his afghan coat around him against the chill from the time winds. He sipped another Martini, watching the lightshow outside, smoking a gold and yellow Sobranie that Iris had given him.

Yes... he remembered the map. It was one of Vince's most treasured possessions. Wherever he went the map went with him. It was too precious to be left in the safe on the houseboat. Glister remembered how the lines and colours on that strangely thick vellum had shimmered and morphed, as if the map was a living thing. Green lights sparked up here and there among the pulsing contours of that chart...

'The souls of all the Martians on Earth,' Glister said. 'That's what the map showed. Where all the Martians were hiding.'

26

'Quite,' said Panda, sitting right beside him. 'And if your Mr Cosmos is retiring, then we need the map off him.'

'But… Vince left everything behind,' said the dwarf. 'All of his outfits and jewellery… everything is still on Earth.'

'We need to know where he might have hidden stuff,' said Panda urgently. 'His bank accounts, his safety deposit boxes.'

Glister shook his head. 'He gave everything away. Every last penny. That's what I found so alarming, before we set off into space. He left himself penniless, as if he knew he was never coming back.'

Panda frowned. Then he hopped off up the gangway to tell Iris. She craned her ear to listen above the screeching of the bus engines and the ear-splitting music from the speakers. Then she nodded firmly and brought the bus in to land.

Next thing, they were emerging from the swirling Maelstrom into a London street. A back street with boarded windows and a great deal of litter swirling about in the stiff breeze. 'You've brought me home!' cried Glister, pleased despite himself. He had really started to think he'd be stuck on that arid desert world for the rest of his life.

Iris came hurrying down the aisle, suddenly wearing bondage trousers and a tattered tartan frock coat held together with safety pins. 'Yes, but not quite in your time, Mr Glister. We've taken you back a handful of years… To 1976.'

She opened the bus' doors and the background London street noise came washing in, making Glister feel instantly at home. 'What happened in 1976?' he frowned.

Panda nudged him, and urged him outside. 'It's all right. Iris has got a smashing plan for retrieving the map…'

1976 was the year of Wembley, Glister realized, suddenly, as he saw exactly where they were. The vast stadium was filled to capacity on the day the bus had deposited them, and Glister remembered how that eighty thousand-strong crowd had queued up especially to see Vince.

It was the largest single audience Vince ever played to and the day had been a fraught one all round.

'Hey! I'm here already!' Glister cried, as he joined the queue with Iris and Panda. The Vince fans spared him only the most cursory of glances. He was glad none of them recognized him. Many were plastered in Vince make-up and sporting home-made Vince costumes. Others were made up in the punkish fashion of the time. Vince was one of the few older stars of Glam who had still been respected by the nascent punks, Glister remembered. Though it was during this 1976 tour, with all its theatrical pomp and excess, that that particular tide had started to turn...

Oh, god. It was the Galactic Pharaoh Tour, wasn't it? Glister shuddered at the very thought. The tour with the fifteen contortionist dancers dressed as lizard people. And the hundred-foot tall golden sphinx with angel wings that extended during the final number. Resulting in the electrocution of several fans in the front rows during a rainy night in Glasgow. That disastrous piece of hydraulics in that monstrously self-indulgent tour that even Vince had wound up regretting bitterly by the end.

So that's what we're here to see, thought Glister miserably. I've been whizzed back through time three years in order to witness Vince's most witless spectacle. And, here at Wembley, the final concert appearance he made in the UK to date.

'Oh, I hear it's just awful,' Panda was grinning. 'Just shockingly bad. All the band abseil down from the top of the stadium, all of them clutching their instruments... and then, as they play the introduction, a giant golden egg is rolled out onto the stage by the dancing lizards. And then, as the first song starts, the egg cracks open and Vince himself climbs out, dressed in gold, with his hair apparently in flames, singing a B side from 1968.'

'It sounds ghastly,' said Iris, with relish.

Glister groaned. He remembered the whole thing only too well. He and Poppy Munday had begged and pleaded with Vince during the months of planning that had gone into this tour. Please don't sing only

28

your most obscure tracks! Please don't have a gigantic sphinx and everybody on Kirby wires! Please don't give into your wildest, most self-indulgent ideas about how to stage a stadium concert!

But there had been no reasoning with him.

They took their seats in the stadium, and all three were impressed by the size of the crowd. 'Eighty thousand!' Panda exclaimed. 'Just think how popular he must be!'

'And think how unpopular he is just about to be,' moaned Glister. 'He's about to disappoint and turn off all of this lot. Just wait for the long monologues about aliens and the thirty minute drum solo while Vince changes into his kabuki costume. I don't know why he bothered. No one more than twenty feet away could see him anyway!'

The crowd were chanting enthusiastically, carried away by the atmosphere as the sun set over Wembley and the stage lit up green and gold. Heavy drapes concealed the elaborate set design.

'Let's sit through the first half,' Iris said. 'Until the interval. Then we'll sneak backstage and get what we came for...' She eyed Glister meaningfully. 'And that's where you come in. You can show us where the map is concealed.'

'But...' Glister spluttered. 'You think it's here? You think he took it with him wherever he went?'

She nodded. 'Yes, I do. I don't think he let it go very far at all. It was too important. And I think you're the one with whom he entrusted it, Mr Glister.'

Glister muttered to himself as the audience started whooping more energetically and the lightshow over Wembley intensified. Something was happening at the front of the stage...

The show started up.

The first half lasted just over an hour.

It was as horrible as Glister remembered.

The audience stood dumbstruck at the awfulness of it all.

'Holy fuck,' said Panda.

'Sssh,' said Iris. 'I'm sure it'll get better in the second half.'

'It won't,' Glister growled.

Suddenly Iris was out of her seat, clutching Panda to her bosom, and pushing the dwarf along ahead of her. 'It's true,' sighed Iris, jogging along, feeling slightly crushed and claustrophobic as they fought with the crowd. 'I think Vince has lost it by now, hasn't he? He seemed so uninterested in his own songs. He was caught up in the spectacle of it all... like the performers up there and all the special effects were playing out some kind of intense psychodrama of his own...'

'It looked like crap,' said Panda.

They struggled through the concrete tunnels, where disappointed punters were queuing for hotdogs and beer. They heard some moaning about the lack of hit tunes and others complaining about too many. It seemed that Vince could please no one with this show.

It took them a little longer than planned to get round the back and into the security area. Mr Glister realized that this was one of his functions. He was the Trojan horse for this strange duo. Only he could smuggle them behind the scenes. As they approached the security guards he was seized with doubt. Who were these time travelers after all? Why was he trusting them like this? Was it just that he was grateful for being rescued from the former planet Glam?

'Why should I help you?' he said, out of the corner of his mouth.

Iris raised a surprised eyebrow. 'Because the fight must go on, Mr Glister. If Vince gives up in 1979, then someone has to carry on, don't they?'

'I suppose so,' he mumbled. He knew the old bat was right. The Martians were still out there, weren't they? Undeterred and still keen to rule the Earth. And if Vince had given up, who was going to take his place? 'Okay, I'll get you the map,' he said.

But they hadn't counted on Poppy Munday.

'What are you doing back here?' she cried. 'And who are these two?' She stared incredulously at Iris and Panda.

The three of them had been caught red-handed by Vince's P.A as they rummaged about in the dressing room. Vince was elsewhere. Curled into a foetal shape, meditating in the toilet. The noise of his chanting could be heard in the dressing room as the interlopers hunted through scattered belongings. They were so caught up in their frantic task that they hadn't even noticed Poppy come in.

'I thought you were helping with the set change,' she frowned at Glister. 'Didn't I just see you out there, struggling with the space dragon's tail?'

'Er, yes,' said Glister, blushing. 'But I'm – erm – here as well.' He stared at Poppy's innocent, doll-like face and sighed. He'd always adored this girl. Though he could never have told her anything of the sort, of course. Here she was just three years ago, and it seemed like a lifetime. Back when they were all together. He remembered that blue and orange striped stretchy turtleneck she had worn back then. He sighed and glanced sideways at Iris and Panda, seeing again how bizarre they must look to Penny. The only thing was to come clean, wasn't it?

Before he could speak, Iris said, 'I'm a groupie, chuck. I'm here because I'm in love with Vince. You've caught me! Oh no!' She threw up her beringed hands in mock horror.

'And I'm a groupie, too,' said Panda, eyeing Poppy beadily.

Poppy looked worried. 'You really shouldn't be back here. Our security's meant to be better than that. After all the death threats and so on that Vince has had...'

'I imagine that the Galactic Pharaoh tour has upped the number of death threats considerably,' mused Panda.

Poppy nodded unhappily. 'That's because Vince is a visionary. He's way ahead of his time. But how do you know about the increased number of death threats?'

'Because I've just seen the show,' said Panda. 'And it was shit.'

31

'Come on,' said Glister. 'We better get what we came for and get out of here.'

'Wait!' said Poppy. 'What are you doing?'

'We need the map,' Iris snapped. She wasn't in the mood now, to quibble with this girl. 'You know where it is, don't you? The map that shows where the Martians are hiding?'

Poppy gasped. 'How do you know about that? Mr Glister... how could you tell anyone about..?'

Glister tried to explain. 'I'm from the future, Poppy. I'm from 1979.'

Poppy gasped again. 'The world's still here in 1979?' she asked. 'Well, that's something.'

'It's a grimmer place,' said Glister. 'And Vince has retired from showbiz. He has returned to the stars...'

Poppy's eyes were out on stalks. 'No! He can't! He can't do that...!'

Glister nodded sadly. 'I'm afraid it's true. I went with him myself, to his home world. And I watched him walk alone into the howling desert. In 1979 Vince has renounced Glam Rock and the Music Biz and his calling on planet Earth. We can't rely on him forever, Poppy.'

The girl looked horrified. She struggled with her feelings and didn't seem to know what to say. Then she blurted out, 'You're telling me this today! In the middle of the most important concert of the tour...!'

'It's his last concert,' Panda told her. 'The last one he'll ever do. It's so horribly bad that he daren't go out on tour again. Or even go out in public much more. They bottle him off the stage in the second half. Just wait and see.'

'Oh my god,' said Poppy.

'He goes off to Holland for the rest of the Seventies,' Panda went on. 'And there he records a trilogy of ground-breaking experimental folk rock albums using only instruments made out of gourds. And then, in 1979, he pops off into space and is never seen or heard from again.'

'I'm afraid it's true,' sighed Iris. 'We have seen the future of pop.'

'They know what they're talking about,' Glister told Poppy gently. 'Especially about those experimental gourds.'

'Fuck's sake,' said Poppy, looking stricken. 'And he leaves the Earth at the mercy of the Martians?'

'We're afraid so,' said Panda.

Poppy thought for a moment or two, and seemed to come to a decision. She marched over to all the stage costumes and the folding cases that held unaccountable amounts of make-up and glitter. She reached inside a secret, pull-out compartment and produced a small scroll of paper. 'Take this,' she said.

They were interrupted by a knock at the door. 'Five minutes,' came the prompt.

Everyone froze.

Mr Glister said, 'That's *me* out there!'

There was a pause and then the knock came again. 'Vince?' asked Mr Glister's voice.

Everyone looked at the three-years-older Mr Glister. 'Tell him to go away,' he told Poppy.

'I-it's okay, Mr Glister,' Poppy called out. 'Vince is just about ready...'

'Is he all right?' asked the gruff voice beyond the door.

'H-he's fine. Raring to go.'

There was another pause, as if the Glister on the other side of the door was thinking. Then the doorknob twisted and in he stepped. The earlier Mr Glister was wearing a Galactic Pharaoh Tour t-shirt and a troubled expression. 'It's a disaster, isn't it?' he said, sotto voce. Then he realized that he and Poppy weren't alone in the room.

He saw Iris and Panda first. And then he saw himself, three years older and slightly balder. 'Fuck me!' he shouted.

The senior Glister looked shocked. 'I don't remember this happening!'

'That's because you've buggered up the time continuum!' snarled Panda.

'What about the Bellinivitch Time Limitation Effect?' Iris asked crossly.

'Don't let them touch each other!' Panda shouted. 'There'll be a huge fucking explosion!'

Iris shot him a glance. 'You're swearing a lot in this story, Panda.'

Both Mr Glisters were staring at each other, and rounding on each other like two diminutive boxers.

Poppy shouted, 'Panda says don't touch each other!'

'I don't intend to!' yelled the younger Glister. 'But what the hell's going on?'

Just at this moment Vince came out of the toilet, wearing his Pharaoh costume from the start of the second act. 'Two Glisters!' he exclaimed.

'I can explain,' Iris said, waving the rolled-up map about.

The younger Glister gasped at this. 'She's got the map, Vince! The special map!'

'I think we'd better make a run for it,' Panda chivvied Iris.

'You gave this to her,' Glister accused his older self.

'You're right!' Glister said. 'I've been helping them!'

Vince looked shocked. 'How could you? Who are these people?'

But Iris and Panda were already making good their escape, with the special map planted firmly down Iris's cleavage.

'Call security!' shouted the junior Glister.

'This is no good,' drawled Vince in a troubled voice. Poppy wondered what he had taken to keep him so calm.

The senior Glister shouted him, 'It's all your fault, Vince! You threw away your whole career and so someone else has to take over looking after planet Earth!'

Vince looked surprised. 'That old woman? That small bear?'

'MIAOW,' said Poppy, looking terribly worried all of a sudden. 'They've been sent by MIAOW, haven't they? That's who they're working for!'

The younger Glister turned angrily on his older self. 'Is that true?' he yelled. 'Have you sold us out to MIAOW?'

The older Glister didn't have time even to think about this, before he was assailed by his own furious self. And just as Glister punched Glister in the nose there was a pretty fucking big explosion in the dressing room deep under Wembley.

As they ran away through the concrete tunnels, both Iris and Panda heard its scintillating echoes. 'It's the Bellinivitch Time Limitation Effect!' Iris shouted.

'Fuck!' said Panda. 'Are they all dead?'

As they ran Iris was imagining bits of truculent dwarf flying far and wide. She imagined time punching a crack in the sky. 'I don't think so,' she said.

They heard footsteps running behind them then, and turned to see the senior Glister hurrying up to them.

'Are you okay?' Panda asked. 'We heard a very loud bang.'

'I'm fine,' he said. 'The explosion thingy was enough to distract them, and for me to get away. Fuck me, though. This time travel thing is a bit of a chew on, though, isn't it?'

'Certainly is,' said Panda.

'Hurray anyway,' said Iris. 'We got the map! Mission accomplished!'

They turned the corner and found they were amongst the milling crowds again, as fans started returning to their seats outside. Everyone was buying up extra bottles of pop and beer, ready to lob them at the stage. A tannoy voice was announcing the second half of the show.

'Sounds like Vince is okay to perform,' said Glister.

35

'Time will return to the way it was before,' said Iris. 'Everything is back on course.'

'Do we have to sit through the rest of it?' Panda pulled a face.

'Of course!' smiled Iris. 'It's an historic moment in pop history! And besides, I'm dying to see the bit when Vince flies up to the top of the sphinx and the sphinx's wings spread out and they soar over everyone's heads...'

'Yeah, that bit's great,' Glister admitted. 'I wouldn't mind seeing that again.'

Iris told them, 'You two get back to our seats. I'll fetch us some drinks, eh?'

They complied, but Panda cast a glance back at Iris, whom he knew was up to something. She had that note in her voice that meant she was about to do something mysterious, nefarious and the kind of thing she didn't want the others to know about.

Blithely Iris shouldered up to the bar and asked for three gin and tonics in plastic glasses.

The woman in the Vince Cosmos T shirt behind the makeshift bar had a livid scar down one cheek and her hair was cut in a very severe bob.

Iris recognized her at once.

'Mida Slike,' she nodded, as the woman poured out the gin. 'The head of MIAOW herself. I am honoured.'

Mida Slike pursed her lips as she twisted the cap off the tonic bottle. 'This is an important transaction, Operative Wildthyme. I had to do it myself.'

Iris nodded, and glanced around at the thinning crowds. Then she leaned forward and produced the rolled up map from inside her cardigan. Mida's eyes lit up greedily at the sight of it.

'Give me the thing, first,' Iris snapped, as Mida reached out.

The head of MIAOW sighed. Then she reached under the bar and produced a small, clouded memory crystal.

Iris nodded. 'Everything's on here? All the evidence? Everything to do with my work for MIAOW? There's nothing else to show that I ever worked for you?'

'That's it,' muttered Mida. 'From this moment, we set you free, Iris. You are no longer an operative of ours.'

'Good,' said Iris, with feeling. Then she handed the map of Martian souls over to Mida Slike and the organization known as MIAOW.

'Thank you, Iris. We shall make good use of this.'

Iris turned to go. 'I'm sure you will.'

Then a series of cascading, doom-laden chords from Jack Bronson's guitar heralded the start of the first number of Vince's second act.

There was a huge roar from the crowd as they hefted their bottles ready for throwing, and Vince took to the stage in Egyptian Pharaoh drag, and Iris Wildthyme quickened her pace in her bondage trousers, keen not to miss a single moment of the show.

Slip Away
Scott Liddell

One of those big American cars drove past. You know the kind, about the length of a cricket pitch and unerringly right-angled. Like the ones I drew as a boy; a long rectangle with a shorter one on top. As far as I knew, cars didn't have curves. But we didn't have a car. Maybe the posh kids drew cars with curves. I didn't know about those; the kids and the cars. You can only aspire to the limit of your knowledge. The posh kids might not be impressed with me having made it all the way to America. But I guess they'd be confused as I am that it seems to be 1959, eleven years before I was born.

It took me a while to notice. I remember my first walk along the busy, well, freeway I think they call it. Lane upon lane of massive cars all progressing like a parade of geometric dinosaurs. I was drawn to a spot on the hill above the road. The foot worn path took me along the back of a giant billboard advertising some car or other. On the grass, just beyond, I was compelled to sit.

The position offered a good view of the road below. I counted eight lanes that only a really mad frog would try to cross. I tried to count the cars but quickly stumbled; there were too many, stretched out in either direction a ribbon of combustion and chrome fins all neatly contained in parallel lines joining at an apparent infinity.

The day passed and I felt relaxed. It was warm and I had nowhere to be and nothing to worry me. Everyone below seemed intent on something or other. The morning sun floated overheard and sunk into hazy evening. I didn't move. I didn't have to; this was all I really wanted to do.

The next day was the same. I don't remember where I slept but the next morning I followed the same path behind the billboard and took my place above the road and another day passed. All the time, I felt free, euphoric even. Another day of warmth and the fewest cares of anyone I could see. That night the same gorgeous sunset descended behind a distant roller-coaster. I smiled broadly at it.

It was only after a week or so that anything at all started to seem strange. I had started absent-mindedly pulling the grass as I sat. By the end of the day I had usually created a bald spot. On maybe the 10th or 11th day, I'm not sure exactly, I noticed that the grass was complete again. I didn't think much of it at first. But then I started to look for it. I made bigger and bigger holes in the grass and each time the hole was gone the next day.

I never really was that worried. There was a curiosity but nothing that ever got close to concern. So the grass came back. It felt like it should. Then I put some of the grass I pulled into my pocket. I think maybe I had forgotten I had done it the first time as I don't remember looking for it. A few days after I did it again. The next day I looked for it and it was gone. Again, no great concern, just a shrug and an 'oh well'.

I maybe did this a few more times before I started to wonder what happened to the grass. It seemed natural that I had taken it out at some point over the night. But then I realised, over a number of weeks, that I never saw the night. No memory of it. Nothing. The day drifted to some sort of end and then, well, I was back on the path at the start of the day. I assumed I must be going somewhere. It wasn't a massive worry, after all, I arrived safe back in my place the next day. Didn't really matter, did it? Each day was so pleasant and full of vibrant life. I didn't have a care in the world.

One of those big American cars drove past. It was a baby blue Edsel. I don't know how I knew it was an Edsel but it was. A very distinctive shape and there weren't many of them. I watched it each evening until, eventually, I realised it was the same car each time. I started to try to work out what the last memory of each day was.

Each day passed with the same serenity but as evening approached I watched the cars and started to feel, for the first time in the many weeks I had been coming to the spot, a slight sense of foreboding. I was putting myself under pressure to find the Edsel in the sea of cars, to try to remember what came next, to sense the end of the remembered day.

The Edsel always approached on the inside lane next to the pavement. It drew up behind a much larger truck in the lane outside it and...

And the next day I'd try again. I'd always see the truck first and the Edsel approaching to undertake it. I'd watch as the Edsel closed and then disappeared from my view behind the truck and then...

Day after day I forced myself to concentrate on that moment. But nothing. I could always remember the Edsel disappearing behind the truck. Lots of those big American cars drove past. But the Edsel never did. I never saw it emerge from behind the truck.

It became an obsession that ate into my peaceful days. And I could only think about that moment. That moment in the early evening when my day seems to end and I have no memory of what happens until the day starts afresh. That realisation created others; like the shock had opened my eyes. I decided this must be America, probably East Coast. I could see an amusement park in the distance which I think must be Coney Island. That also felt natural at first. It felt like a form of home at least. It was only when I started to pick out details that suggested *when* it was that things began to feel odd. It was the Edsel that gave me the first clue. I began to realise that it was not a car I'd ever seen on the road before. Although it didn't feel overly strange, I began to sense that perhaps I was not where I belonged and, after a while, not *when* I belonged. It took more concentration than I had at first. I tried to remember my birth date. I didn't know it. 'Oh well'. Then it came to me. 1970. I was born in 1970. And this is...

One of those big American cars drove past. This is before 1970. I wasn't sure at first but day after day I hunted for detail from my position on the hill. The cars. The people. Hats and A-Line skirts. And then, one day, instead of walking behind the billboard, I walked in

40

front of it. It announced it huge letters *'New for 1959'*.

It is eleven years before I was born and I spend each day beside the road watching the sun sailing over Coney Island. And as the sky starts to darken I watch. And I watch. Until.

The big, baby-blue American car approaches. The Edsel. It cruises up alongside the truck and disappears behind and...

...from the other side of the truck a large red bus appears and comes to an abrupt halt. As does everything and everyone around it.

I sit and stare for a while at the static world in front of me. A figure climbs down from the cab of the bus and starts making its way through the stationary cars on the road towards me. A much smaller figure walks behind. By the time the figure had reached the bottom of the hill I could see it was a woman. With her was a small... panda? She struggled a bit up the climb. As she approached a broad smile spread across her face. Still nothing moved below.

'Lovely evening, chuck.'

I suddenly realised how long it had been since I had spoken to someone and froze.

'Don't worry, I know this is all a wee bit odd. Take your time love. There's no rush. No one is going anywhere.'

I open my mouth to reply but only managed a vague noise.

'Buh...'

'You've started to wonder what the hell is going on? Bet you have...'

'The car and well, the grass and... you... you have a bus? And a toy panda?'

I was pleased to get some words out finally. She was soothing. This evidently was entirely normal to her. The panda made a loud tutting noise.

'Lovely Bus, isn't it? Want to see it?'

'You mean... go down? To the road?'

'Nothing to get in your way at the mo.'

She was jolly and relaxed. This wasn't at all unnatural to her.

'Yes, everything has... stopped. I...'

'Bet you're wondering where you are?'

She was right, I was. And yet, I didn't want to move. The hill was will still the place I was supposed to be.

'Come on laddie. Let's go for a walk.'

I really didn't want to go.

'Why... why did you call me laddie?' I asked, trying to waste time, to put off the need to move.

I thought at first she hadn't heard, or was ignoring me. Instead of replying, she picked up her bag and, after some rummaging and clinking noises, she produced a mirror, which she handed to me, without a word

I took it – and leapt back quickly, shocked to see the face of a young boy. I seemed to be ten or so years old.

'I... that... I was born in 1970.'

'You were that, you were that. Look love, come with me. I'll explain everything on the Bus.'

For the first time since I started spending time on the hill I felt very unsettled.

'No, I don't want to go on the bus.'

'I know, I know. But, well, that's the only way we can get on with this.'

'What do you mean?'

I could tell my voice was starting to sound fraught and, for the first time, I heard the sound of a young boy.

'Look around you, chuck. Everything's stopped hasn't it?'

'Yes.'

'Well, it's not going to start again until we get on the Bus.'

'But tomorrow comes, when the, when the...'

'When the big blue car comes?'

'Yes, how did you know that?'

The panda moved round in front of me and stretched out a

42

small hand.

'Come with me young man.' said the Panda.

'No, I'm fine here thanks.'

The little black creature seemed to be getting impatient.

The woman was right, tomorrow appeared not be coming. Nothing was moving and it should already be tomorrow. I had seen the Edsel go behind the truck. But still I didn't want to go down to the road.

'You're not going to come, are you?' Her voice sounded resigned.

'I know you won't understand, love, but it's much better for you if you come down to the Bus. But I know it's hard. It usually is. So, how about we explain? That be OK?'

I looked up at the orangey sky and the golden light that glinted off the people and cars below. And the roller-coaster car, frozen in the distance. The sun wasn't going down any more.

'OK, I... I'd like to understand.'

She sighed deeply. Something had saddened her. She spoke quietly.

'OK, if you don't like what you hear, don't say I didn't warn you.'

I got the impression this wasn't something she enjoyed doing. Not that I knew what it was. She turned to the Panda.

'Have you ever heard the phrase 'life flashing before your eyes'?' he said.

'Like what people say you see just before you die?'

'That's the one.' I sensed some relief in his voice. But that quickly turned to hesitation again.

'You know, this isn't the easiest thing to explain. Are you sure you won't get on the Bus?'

If anything, I was now a lot more worried and even less likely to accompany the weird woman and her bizarre little creature onto a bus that had appeared out of nowhere and stopped time.

'Yes. I'm sure.'

The woman leant down into her bag and pulled out a packet of crumpled cigarettes and a lighter. After several attempts with the lighter she went back to her bag for some matches.

'Fire isn't too keen on places like this. Never really understood why. I'm sure there some sort of sub-atomic mumbo-jumbo to account for it. '

The large match flickered dimly into life and she hurriedly lit the cigarette and took and a long smoky breath. It looked like she needed it.

'Right. Bugger this. I'll tell you it all but I warn you now, you won't like it.'

She paused, stared at the dying end of the cigarette and drew on it as hard as she could to keep it burning, without success. It died slowly and she cast it away onto the grass with a resigned flick or her hand.

'You ever wonder why people say that life flashes before their eyes just before they die?'

'Well, I suppose I assumed it was just a saying.'

The woman nodded.

'Yes, well, it used to be just a saying, then some idiot got themselves killed and an even bigger idiot decided to try to stop that happening again. I really have no idea why these people insist on tinkering.'

I must have looked very bemused at this point. The woman turned to the Panda, who raised an eyebrow at her.

'Panda, you'd better explain this, it's too bloody, aaargh...'

The Panda looked like he had been waiting patiently for the invite.

'Please excuse my friend, this situation, well, upsets her somewhat. I would, of course, be delighted to explain.'

The woman wandered off and continued to fail to light a cigarette.

The Panda took a deep breath. His fur seem to puff out a little.

'It's really very simple dear boy. Simple if, well, unfortunate.'

The Panda moved closer and his tone dropped to a whisper, a late night DJ trying not to wake the listeners.

'Dear boy, you probably don't know it, but there are people, like Iris there, who can, how shall I put it? Travel in time.'

'Like on the TV?'

'Well, yes, you may have seen similar things happening on TV, the real thing is far more impressive.'

'So, the bus...'

The Panda smiled. 'Yes, good, the Bus, that's how we get about.' he continued.

'Well, one of those time traveller types sadly met an unfortunate end. A simple accident, was electrocuted by some faulty wiring. As ever with these things, a needless death but someone thought it a little too needless.'

'I'm sorry, I...' I was confused.

'It's a simple idea, if you can travel in time then why get killed by an accident? If you could, at the point of your death, pop back in time a little you could perhaps avoid what was about to kill you.'

It was making more sense generally but wasn't clearing up what it had to do with me.

'So, this *supposedly* clever fellow came up with a device that could detect when someone was about to die and then send you far enough back in time to give you a chance to get out of whatever it is that is about to kill you. When they installed the Point of Death Loopback Mechanism – or Looper, for short – they hooked it up to everything that lived. The theory was that if some people who couldn't time travel got a quick recap of their life it would do them no harm. Except...'

The woman sensed my confusion and, with an apparent growing impatience, butted in.

'Panda you don't half go on! Except it doesn't bloody work does it? Bloody idiot. It's a nice idea though, you go all the way to the start and flash very quickly all the way through your life again. It happens so quickly that you only pick up bits and pieces as you go and you're back dying before anyone notices you were away.'

'What use it that to anyone who doesn't know what's going on?'

The more ridiculous the story got the braver I was getting.

'Good question.'

I received this praise with what I suspect was unnecessary and misplaced pride.

'As Panda said, if you don't know what's going on it doesn't really matter, you just, well, die.'

'Well I don't know what's going on!'

'You were warned that you might not like this! Don't go all Mr. Confused on me now.'

The woman was getting irate. Detecting this, the Panda stepped across her and continued in a quieter tone.

'It's really very simple. The system detects you are about to die and sends you back in time to give you a chance to get out of whatever it is that is about to kill you.'

My glazed look obviously didn't give either of them impression that I was following any of this and, crucially, I had no idea what any of this had to do with me. 'But what does this have to do... with me.'

I hesitated because I had a sudden concern that I might have an inkling of the answer.

'Yes, well. The trouble is, the system is rubbish. It has to guess you're about to die and then send you back. It doesn't always get it right and people survive...'

'...and blab?'

'Now you're getting it, yes, they blab and, every now and then, the system breaks down entirely.'

'So people don't go back through their life. They just die?'

The woman face sank with a mix of relief and despair.

'Yes love, yes, but to be honest, that's not a major issue.'

The Panda threw her a scornful glance.

I could tell she was getting exasperated. She was playing with

46

her lighter with more and more agitation. Perhaps in need of a cigarette but, I guessed, more uncomfortable with what she was telling me. She sighed and continued in a much quieter, softer voice.

'The real problem times are when things get confused and people end up reliving other people's lives.'

She looked at me intently. I could tell she wanted me to make all the necessary connections without her actually having to say them. I was almost there. I could tell she was holding her breath. Her knuckles whitened.

'Let me see if I understand you. What you're saying is that I'm about to die and I'm currently living someone else's life?'

'Yes!' her breath burst out punctuating what she considered to be the end of her explanation.

The Panda looked pleased too; he brushed himself down as if preparing to leave. I didn't really know what to say next. She filled the space for me.

'Although, I'm afraid, yours is the worst possible kind. You're living someone else's life and they are living in yours. It's stuck in a loop, you must have noticed that.'

'I suppose I did but, well, it wasn't all that obvious at first.'

'It wouldn't be. You adopt enough of the consciousness of the other person to feel relaxed in the part of their life you are living. Part of you became a happy go lucky ten year old without a care in the world when...'

'When I'm really...?'

She reached over and held my hand. 'Yes, I'm very sorry to say chuck, you're dying.'

'And the boy?'

Her lips pursed and twisted her face into an anguished grimace.

'I don't know where he is in your life, someone else has jumped into his loop to get him. But, well, you know how your day ends with the Edsel disappearing?'

'Yes.'

'So does his life.'

'That's why I never saw any more?'

There was something very odd about a story that got ever more senseless just as it was starting to make more sense.

'Sadly love, there's no more of his life to live. That's the weirdest malfunction of all. You don't often get people stuck in the lives of those that died in the past.'

'And is he... down there now?'

She paused like she didn't want to answer.

'He is, behind the truck. He fell off his bike and onto the road. That's why you've never gone down near the road...'

It was now making as much sense as it could, given the madness I was listening to. The sense wasn't helping all that much, however. In the space of a few minutes my life had gone from simply confusing to almost over.

'And if I get on that bus with you, I go back to my life and, well, die?'

'I'm afraid so, love' the woman replied, no longer inclined to break anything gently.

'And if I stay here?'

'I'd love it if you could.'

She put her hand on my shoulder; I could smell cigarettes and the alcohol from perfume.

'Yes I can. You go away and I'll go back to living the same carefree day every day. Seems to me to be a better choice than dying.'

'But it's not living either.'

'You could have fooled me!' My voice rose with increasing desperation as my life depended on winning this debate.

'It did, yes, it did.'

I had now gone beyond desperation into survival panic.

'OK, so, if I'm stuck in some malfunction, you can surely do something to stop me dying in the real world? That's the point of this... machine, isn't it?'

'I would if I could. But, well, it's not like I can just push you out the way of a bullet. You have an inoperable brain tumour.'

'Why should I believe you?'

The Grim Reaper had appeared with a glittery handbag, pack of Sobranies and a small stuffed Panda, and whilst I still had any choice... I had to choose to live. Whatever that meant.

She thought for a while, working out her tactics. Trying to find a way to get me to accept my own imminent death.

'How about I show you?'

'Show me what? Let me guess, your bus? I'm not going to fall for that. I get on that I'm as good as dead.'

I walked away from her, further up the hill.

'Right! Wait there. What am I saying, where else are you going to go?'

She seemed to amuse herself briefly but quickly started muttering angrily again.

'I don't have bloody time for this. You try to do people favours and...'

She got up and dusted the grass off herself. Fifty yards down the hill she shouted back.

'There are mints in the bag if you want one, won't be a mo'.'

I didn't want a mint. I wanted the day to end as it always had for weeks. I wanted the day to start with the same sunny optimism and the skip along the road and behind the billboard. The static sunset taunted me. I watched her get on the bus. It disappeared but almost immediately returned. She emerged moments later. Arriving back at the top of the hill she was badly out of breath.

'Here.' She handed me something and spluttered down onto the grass. 'It's a video camera. Watch the video.'

I flipped open the small screen and pushed the play button. The machine clicked and whirred, the screen crackled and a scene appeared.

There was a dimly lit room. In the centre, a man lay motionless in a bed. A group of people sat round the bed in a circle. A woman, nearest the top of the bed was holding the man's hand. On the opposite side, a nurse was attending a drip. Various machines glowed red into the murk. Flowers sat dying in a vase. One of the people got up and went to leave. Another stood up and they embraced. The dim light caught tears as the rolled down the face and off onto the shiny floor. The door opened and a man in a panama hat entered holding a large bunch of flowers. The family turned and looked bemused.

'Is that me in the bed?'

'Yes, that's you.'

'And, the people are my family and they're...'

'Sitting patiently, waiting for you to slip away.'

'How long have they been waiting?'

'I'd like to lie to you, but I can't. All your time in this existence has been brief moments for them.'

'So if I stay here forever they won't notice.'

'No, eventually all time must move on. You will prolong their vigil. You're in a lot of pain. They are watching you suffer. You need to come back on the Bus with me.'

'But I want to live.'

'I know, I know. But in the real world, your family need you to die, for their sake – as well as yours.'

I clicked the camera shut and handed it to her.

'I can see why just getting on the bus would have been easier... for the both of us. Thank you. Thank you for telling me the truth.'

The unexpected thanks seemed to make her more uncomfortable.

'I'm only doing what I need to. There are so few of us to can jump in and help with this kind of thing. We all need to take our turn until they've shut the thing down for good. Although, I won't mind waiting a good while for another go.'

'Yes, yes. I can imagine.'

I sat for a while and stared at the sun frozen in its arc. If it was to be my last sight, I had got lucky. I had breathed the air of 1950's America as a young boy full of hope and vigour. I had seen a family who loved me. I knew things that very few people ever came to know. And, unlike so many, I was able to choose the moment of my death. But somehow it still wasn't enough.

'Can I ask one thing of you?'

'You can ask love, but I can't promise...'

'I want to save the boy.'

'No, no, that's out the question.'

'You said that you couldn't push me out the way of a bullet. But I guess I could push the boy away from the Edsel.'

'I... I just... we're not...'

'Look, it's a very simple. You help me to save the boy and I'll get on the bus. Boy dies. I'll stay here.'

'But what about your family.'

'My family would want me to save him too.'

'Bloody hell.'

'Does that mean you'll do it?'

'Yes chuck, why not?'

The Panda didn't look happy.

'Iris, really, we really can't...'

'Shush, Panda.'

'Shush? SHUSH?'

The Panda strode off annoyed in the direction of the bus.

'I'm having no part in this.'

I was left alone again with the woman.

'Thank you. Again. Iris.'

'No need for thanks young lad.'

She walked off to the bus with more of a spring in her step than I had seen before. Seemed rule breaking appealed to her.

The people of 1950's New Jersey buzzed around me. They all seemed so neat compared to the world I knew that I was now beginning to remember. Men wore pressed suits. Hats sat atop heavily oiled hair. The women's curls bounced as they waddled in their tight skirts with the clip-clop of kitten heel shoes. The clothes were different but, more

51

than anything, their faces told more about this being a different time. I stared at each person as they passed trying to understand why.

A man stopped at a stall to buy a newspaper. The vendor knew his name and they agonised over baseball before parting with a loud 'see ya'. A young boy dodged through the crowd avidly reading a comic book his jaws working over some heavy-duty gum. People nodded, acknowledged, greeted, the interaction of proximity. There was chatter, voices on the street. Smiles.

They seemed like simple people but they just lived in simpler times, perhaps harder times. What I saw in every face was hope. The hope that comes from the wars being behind them and the promise of progress all around. Machines that did things, technology. An advanced life for a better life. Little did they know that it would just get ever more complicated and the chatter on the streets would die down to a whisper.

They weren't simple, they were childlike. The hope was the same thing that every child has staring expectantly at an exciting future. I felt comfortable among them because, I could see me as a child in their faces; the gaze out the window on Christmas Eve, the excited eyes over the sofa at the TV.

And now, there I was, as a child, with no hope. Yet still calm.

I watched the rest of the film on the tape. The woman by the side of the bed got up and took the flowers from the man. He was tall and tanned, perhaps in his early sixties. They started to talk and the tape finished with a crackle into white noise. Looking up from the camera the sky blinked from dusk to day. Iris had reappeared.

'That was a bloody fankle. Come on.'

'Where?'

'Down the hill?'

'But?'

'Look, this was your idea, I've done enough running about without turning up and actually taking part. You want to do this then *you* have to do this.'

I understood. She was right. It was my idea but something

didn't make sense.

'But, if I'm him then how I can I...?'

'No, you're still you, you're just living his life, probably best you don't let him see you though. Might be a wee bit confusing.'

We walked down to the wide freeway. Cars hurtled past across the eight lanes. It seemed more likely I was going to die trying to save him.

'How are we going to get across?'

'You've not really got the hang of this, have you love?'

The cars all stopped and we picked our way across, the drivers staring motionless and open-mouthed, with their placid intent still etched on their faces.

'This is where he goes off into the road. I'll wait up here out the way. When the Edsel comes, all you need to do is watch for the bike and make sure he doesn't go off into the road.'

One of those big American cars drove past. And then another. And then I saw him. A small figure on the sidewalk, knees splayed wide pumping the pedals. I looked for the Edsel behind me. Its large blue shape loomed like a shark in clear water. I stood by the kerb ready to catch the bike. The car and the boy approached. An old lady walked out a shop with her dog. The dog barked and yelped and with a tug, ripped its leash from the old woman's hand and headed across the sidewalk. The boy on the bike swerved to avoid the dog. I rushed forward to catch him, the bike hit me and I pushed it hard in the opposite direction into the old woman. The boy, the bike and the woman ended in an unceremonious pile. The dog, however, made it out into the road and met untimely end at the wheels of the Edsel. A kerfuffle broke out and I ran. The old woman was demanding the police. The young boy looked dazed.

Iris appeared and shouted. 'Quick! Out of sight!'

I passed her and headed off the pavement and into a nearby garden to hide. I watched as the woman approached the scene to calm everyone down. The old woman gesticulated and the young boy got up and checked his bike. Iris pulled a piece of paper from her handbag and handed it to the young boy. She said a few words in his ear and walked briskly towards me.

'Right then, let's get out of here.'

Out of sight round the corner we both laughed.

'I feel...'

'Yourself?'

'Yeah, I'm me.'

'Well, the boy didn't die so he can't be mixed up in you any more. You're left being who you are, a dog killer. Some hero you are.'

'And bruised an old woman.'

She frowned at me. 'Yes there is that.'

'I suppose you want me to bugger off and die now.'

'Well, if you put it like that, yes.'

We got on the bus. Out of the back window I saw the boy cycle away on his bike.

One of those big American cars drove past. The blue Edsel, finally making its way into the setting Coney Island sun.

The people looked confused.

'I'm sorry, this is a private room.'

'Apologies ma'am'.   The nervousness in his voice was clear through the booming American accent. He took off his large panama hat.

'I brought you these flowers.'

'Do I... do we... know you?'

'No, ma'am, no. I, well, it's kinda hard to explain. I just came here to say thank you to your husband.'

'But he's...'

'Dying, yes, yes, I know ma'am. And I'm mighty sorry. He was... he *is*, a very good man, your husband and I came here so you'd know that, so you'd know what a fine man he is.'

'How? How do you know him?'

'Well ma'am, I'm not rightly sure, but something a lady once told me seems to be true and I promised her I would pay my respects. I just came here to say thank you.'

'For... what?'

'Ma'am, I believe that your husband just this very minute saved my life.'

Low/Profile

From Wackopedia, the free encyclopedia
Article last edited by George Mann

This article is about the David Bowie double album. For other stuff which isn't as good, but which has the same name, see Low/Profile (disambiguation)

 The neutrality of this article is disputed. Relevant discussion may be found on the talk page. Please do not remove this message until the dispute is resolved. (September 2012)

Low/Profile is an infamous[original research] 1977 double album by David Bowie, co-produced by Bowie, Tony Visconti and Iris Wildthyme. It is widely regarded as one of his most influential albums[1] , despite the troubled production history and the fact that only half of the album (*Low*) was ever actually released. It is the first in the 'Berlin Trilogy', a series of three albums which marked Bowie's famed collaboration with Brian Eno.

Contents

- 1 Recording History
  - 1.1 Iris Wildthyme and Panda
  - 1.2 Marlene Dietrich
  - 1.3 The Nemenoids
- Tracklisting
  - Low
  - Profile
- Notable Tracks
  - Always Crashing in the Same Car
  - Be My Wife
  - Art Decade
  - The End of the World Address
  - Juniper
  - The Fallen

Recording history

When Bowie went into the studio in West Berlin to mix what would eventually become his eleventh studio album, he could not have anticipated the momentous events that would transpire in the week that followed. Reports at the time claimed he was feeling tired and down, and looking for a way to reinvigorate himself artistically. [2]

Most of the songs that would make it onto the finished album (*Low*) had already been recorded in France, and the project was to be remounted in West Berlin, chiefly in order to mix the existing songs and work on new, additional material.[3] Berlin at the time was a haven for bohemian artists and musicians, and Bowie hoped that the city and its people would provide fresh inspiration for the project.

Iris Wildthyme and Panda

This inspiration came in the surprising form of Iris Wildthyme and her assistant, the internationally famed[original research] art critic, Panda. Bowie happened upon this enigmatic pair at a late night cabaret, where Ms. Wildthyme was performing a set of anachronistic show standards and pop songs, including numbers from the musical Wicked, the Disney/Pixar film Tangled and Soundgarden's Badmotorfinger[4]. Ms. Wildthyme later claimed in a rare interview that: 'David was so taken with my performance that he approached me after the show and asked me to make a guest appearance on his new record.'[5] Panda has a different recollection of events: 'I think he did it to shut her up. Her caterwauling was so abhorrent that he would have said anything just to get her off the stage.'[5]

Whatever the truth of the matter, Bowie was clearly enamoured with the unusual woman[original research] and she swiftly found herself swept up into his entourage, attending the recording sessions the following day. Panda recalls that the pair (Bowie and Ms. Wildthyme) were still drunk when they rolled up at the studio the next morning.[5] Shortly after arriving, Bowie announced that Ms. Wildthyme was to become co-producer on the new record.

Visconti was reportedly incensed by this unexpected development, but was unable to sway Bowie from his decision.[6]

Before long, Ms. Wildthyme had convinced Bowie to start laying down new tracks, and the project had grown to become a double album. Bowie was excited about the new songs and the new direction, stating that he'd finally found the inspiration he'd been searching for.

Marlene Dietrich

Backing vocals for the new, second half of the album came courtesy of Marlene Dietrich, fresh from providing vocals for Suede's Glorious Today EP in 1992[7]. She had returned to 1970s Berlin in the company of the playwright and actor, Noel Coward, and claimed to have been 'passing the studio' one day, when she overhead 'the most beautiful refrain I'd ever heard. I simply had to be a part of whatever was going on inside.' [citation needed] Bowie was utterly taken with the woman, although Ms. Wildthyme wrote a letter to a friend in 1930s England, a Professor Angelchrist, stating that: 'that dreadful harridan is here. She knows something is going on in Berlin and she's come to stick her hooter in. She's a wily one, that Dietrich.'[8]

Nevertheless, despite this apparent animosity, new tracks flowed freely, and creativity was high. Panda said in a 1996 interview on the subject: 'What you've got to remember is that [Berlin] at that time was a melting pot, not only culturally and artistically, but cosmologically speaking. Things were converging on that city. It was a nexus point. That was Berlin's time; it's moment in history. There was a reason the wall had been built – it wasn't simply a physical representation of the political divisions at work in the country, but a barrier, too, designed to keep things out...What David did with that record...he somehow managed to capture it all on vinyl; the mood of an era, a specific time and place, summed up in a smattering of songs. That's particularly true of *Profile*, the lamentably missing half of the album. A divided record for a divided city.'[5]

The party atmosphere in the studio extended into the long nights, giving way to much drinking, smoking and carousing. Ms. Wildthyme was instrumental in instigating these late night gatherings, during which the band would play back and assess the day's recordings. However, the cracks were beginning to show, and things soon took a turn for the worst. It was during one of these drinking sessions that the first attack occurred. [citation needed]

The Nemenoids

Berlin, it transpired, was a city under siege. A race of alien entities known as the Nemenoids were secretly at large, drawn to Earth – and Berlin in particular – by the sheer intensity of cultural and creative energy being generated by the population there. To the Nemenoids, this energy represented an almost limitless source of food; they would strip Berlin of every modicum of its artistic integrity. Ultimately, they had come to Berlin for the same reason as Bowie: to soak up the cultural atmosphere.[original research]

The creatures manifested in this dimension as spindly humanoids with fleshy wings and grotesque, bird-skull heads.[citation needed] They had engineered a space-time anomaly on the other side of the wall and were using it as a gateway to gain a foothold in our reality. They worked by stealth, coming only at night to feed on the energy of the artists.

Ms. Wildthyme explained all of this to Bowie as they took cover in a broom cupboard at the studio, sitting it out until the first wave of the attack was over. The creatures, she said, had swarmed to the studio because of the music, hungry to consume its vibe.[5]

The following day, during a cigarette break[citation needed], Ms. Wildthyme showed Bowie the devastation wreaked by the marauding monsters. Bowie was utterly appalled by the sight of so many corpses, and the emotional outburst that followed fueled the epic closing track of *Profile*, 'The Fallen', Bowie's tribute to those Berliners who had lost their lives in the attack. The sight of the creatures and what they had done had moved Bowie intensely. It was during the recording of this song that Bowie agreed to help Ms. Wildthyme defeat the Nemenoids, by forging some new material that was so potent – so emotionally powerful – that it would overwhelm the creatures even as they attempted to consume it. [original research]

So it continued: by day creating new music – by night using it as a weapon to hold off and combat the invaders. Most of the city's population was not even aware of the threat they were under, or the terrible battle going on under their noses. Visconti, Eno, Dietrich, Panda, Coward, Bowie and Wildthyme: seven of them against an army of interdimensional beings, hungry for their artistic souls.[citation needed]

On the fifth night following Ms. Wildthyme and Panda's arrival, Panda recalls that Bowie finally began to comprehend what was truly going on. He had not encountered Ms. Wildthyme by accident, that night in the cabaret. Nor had Marlene and Coward arrived by chance. 'Iris was using us as a lure,' said Panda, in 1996. 'She'd pulled us together, this coterie of incredible creative power, locking us up in that studio for days on end. Of course she knew what she was doing. She was luring the Nemenoids in, like moths to a flame. We were the brightest light in that brightest of cities, and the Nemenoids couldn't resist. They flocked to us in their masses, and she was ready: she had the new album to use as a weapon.'[8]

So it was that, on the third consecutive night of attacks, the Nemenoids came en masse, clawing at the studio windows. Bowie and Ms. Wildthyme had planned their countermeasure, however, and they unleashed Profile in all its glory, pumping the soulful music out into the warm Berlin night. The creatures responded rapturously, lapping up the creative energy that radiated from the sound waves, teasing it out, absorbing it into themselves with glorious abandon. Too late, they realised their error, and their gluttony proved their undoing; *Profile* was simply too rich for their alien palates, and with a single, ominous musical note that rang out across the entire city, they expired. The invasion was over.[original research]

In their moment of triumph, however, Bowie and Ms. Wildthyme discovered their loss; the entire second half of the album had been utterly absorbed, consumed by the Nemenoids in their death throes. There was nothing left. The tapes were blank, the equipment burned out.[citation needed]

No one could face remounting the recording the following day, and besides, according to Panda: 'the music was gone. It wasn't as if we could just record it all again. The Nemenoids had consumed it in all its forms. None of us could even remember the notes we'd played. We disbanded quickly after that. It was over.'[5]

61

Bowie released the remaining tracks later that year as *Low*. It is not known whether he ever encountered Iris Wildthyme or Marlene Dietrich again.

Profile remains one of greatest lost recordings of the modern age.[original research]

Tracklisting

Low

Side one

1. 'Speed of Life' – 2:46
2. 'Breaking Glass' (Bowie, Dennis Davis, George Murray) – 1:52
3. 'What in the World' – 2:23
4. 'Sound and Vision' – 3:05
5. 'Always Crashing in the Same Car' – 3:33
6. 'Be My Wife' – 2:58
7. 'A New Career in a New Town' – 2:53

Side two

1. 'Warszawa' (Bowie, Brian Eno) – 6:23
2. 'Art Decade' – 3:46
3. 'Weeping Wall' – 3:28
4. 'Subterraneans' – 5:39

Profile

Side one

1. 'Anomalous Readings' – 3.26
2. 'Resonance' – 5.12
3. 'The End of the World Address' (Bowie, Brian Eno) – 2.45
4. 'Oh, Marlene' – 1.19
5. 'Broken Wheels' – 8.34

Side two

1. 'Nighttime Curiosity' – 4.25
2. 'Juniper' – 2.53
3. 'Black & White' (Bowie, Panda) – 3.47
4. 'The Fallen' – 8.18

Notable Tracks

Main article: David Bowie discography

Always Crashing in the Same Car

The origins of this track have always been shrouded in mystery; some claim it was inspired by the late night tales of Iris Wildthyme[who?] who is said to have regaled the band with stories of distant worlds and other times during the long hours of the Nemenoid siege. It is held that one particular tale – about Marc Bolan (still alive at the time) being caught in a vicious time loop, in which he crashed his car into a tree over and over again – was the true inspiration for the song.

Panda, however, argues it was based on an old shanty sung by Iris as she drove her bus through the vortex.[9] He recalls the original lyrics as follows:

'Always Crashing in the Same Bus'

Every gin
Every gin that I drink
I take it with the tonic (and the fags)
That vortex and the swimming lights
I was never looking left and right
Gah, but I'm always crashing
In the same bus

Panda, I saw you weeping
As I pushed my boot down to the floor
I was chasing round and round that foolish runaway
He must have been adventuring in time once more
Gah, but I'm always crashing
In the same bus

It is not clear who the unnamed subject of the song (the 'runaway') is supposed to be, but many have speculated that it may refer to the mysterious 'El Jefe' [citation needed]

Be My Wife

Marlene Dietrich, who had joined the recordings in Berlin as a backing singer, is said to have had a profound affect on Bowie during the studio sessions[citation needed]. Dietrich was approaching 34 years of age (in her personal timeline) and was stunningly beautiful. Her voice, both soulful and feminine, was known to have powerful mesmerising effects. Whether she purposefully set out to seduce Bowie, or whether it was a simple by-product of her sheer presence, remains a mystery. What's clear is that Bowie most certainly fell under her spell: 'Be My Wife' is perhaps the clearest indicator of this, both a proposition and a heartfelt recognition of unrequited love.

Iris Wildthyme was reportedly furious with Dietrich[citation needed] for 'taking advantage of the boy', although it has been argued by Art Critic Panda that she was exhibiting signs of 'petulance and jealousy' and that: 'what she really wanted was the man to herself. She'd always had a thing about fellas in eyeliner.'[5]

Art Decade

Originally titled 'Art Critic Decade', this track is supposedly an instrumental lamentation by Bowie about the momentous hangover incurred the morning after an all night drinking party with Panda. [citation needed] Iris Wildthyme is purported to have laughed at Bowie when she found him asleep beneath the kitchen table at the back of the studio, and remarked 'It'll take the poor bugger a decade to get over one of Panda's hangovers.' [citation needed]

The End of the World Address

During the night-long siege at the recording studio, when the Nemenoids were launching their major attack, Bowie scribbled a last note to the universe on the back of a torn cigarette packet.[10] He hadn't, it is presumed, expected to survive until morning, and 'The End of the World Address' was intended to be his final statement to the world should he die in the ensuing battle. [citation needed]

Earlier that day Eno had provided a new keyboard melody, although the details of the track are now lost to posterity. Panda recalls that 'it had originally been intended as another purely instrumental track, but as the fight with the aliens raged on outside, Bowie and I settled themselves in the recording booth and laid down a version of the lyrics, read as a statement over the music, each of us taking turns to perform the same words repeatedly to form a loop.' [citation needed]

It is thought that this track, of the many that were consumed by the Nemenoids, was fundamental in the alien's destruction.

Juniper

Panda says of this track that it was 'a response to the sheer amount of gin consumed by Iris [Wildthyme] during the recordings'. Legend has it that Bowie, upon waking up one morning on the studio floor beside a prone and unconscious Ms. Wildthyme, was 'induced to vomit by the impossible intensity of the woman's breath and the terrible reek of juniper' that emanated from her. Inspired to write of his experience, he went immediately to the recording booth and thrashed out this 'rocky acoustic number, full of rage and brimstone.'

The Fallen

'The Fallen' is Bowie's tribute to the dead of Berlin, and specifically to those who had succumbed to the Nemenoids' brutal assault on the city. It is thought that over a hundred people died during the three day invasion, despite the clandestine nature of the alien's attack and the fact that not a single newspaper, radio station or television network published a statement or reported sighting of one of the creatures. The sharp rise in civilian deaths was instead attributed to a new strain of influenza, and the alien invasion was never officially acknowledged.

It was during the aftermath of the first wave assault that Bowie and Iris Wildthyme are said to have happened upon a scene of absolute devastation during a cigarette break; strewn corpses littered around a fountain in a square close to the studio. Bowie was filled with such sorrow that he uttered the words: 'the bleak and ignored remnants of the fallen/cast like pallid stones into the fountain of the world.' The song grew from this sorrowful couplet to become the defining track of *Profile*; an eight minute masterpiece of soaring guitar and piano, with Bowie's plaintive, funereal vocals laid subtly over the top.

Release History, Critical Reception and Legacy

When Low was released in 1977 it was in a much curtailed format, with only the first half of the album surviving intact. This proved no barrier, however, to an unsuspecting public, nor to critics, who (almost) universally praised the new record.

Melody Maker proclaimed it 'a triumph of modern musical art,' but ironically suggested the record perhaps suffered from a shorter-than-anticipated running time, and that: 'the ideas and innovative melodies on show might have benefited from further exploration.'

Similarly, Record Buyer International said it was 'a remarkable piece of work, but one is somehow left with the feeling that we're not getting the full story.'

The album sleeve played a visual pun, showing a profile shot of Bowie beneath the title, 'Low'. This was clearly a reference to the lamented lost half of the album, which has now come to be regarded as near mythical in fan circles, being heralded as one of the great, lost recordings of modern music. Much like the fans of old, deleted television shows (such as Doctor Who, Dad's Army, Callan), enthusiasts haunt the archives of sound engineers and record companies, or search the internet daily for word of any recovered snippets of sound.

In 2004 Spun magazine ran a retrospective article on Bowie's career, and heralded *Low* as the musician's single greatest achievement. The journalist in question, Arven Jones, went on to discuss the 'other, unreleased recordings' made at the time, clearly eluding to the lost *Profile* tracks. He claimed to have heard third generation copies of the original sound recordings in a garage in Walthamstow, played to him by 'an odd bag lady in a funny hat, who produced them on reels from a Morrison's carrier bag and proceeded to sit and smoke while the music played, an introspective expression on her face.' Fans immediately went into uproar and the magazine was inundated with letters and emails; the magazine later put out a statement saying that the recordings were simply earlier takes of the same songs from Low, and that Jones had been unable to retain any copies. Conspiracy theorists doubt the validity of this last statement, however, believing that it was a manufactured cover up by the editor of the magazine, and that what Jones had been privy to were, in fact, rare recordings of the long lost tracks. [original research]

Consequently, in 2006, nearly a minute's worth of instrumental music turned up on the internet, thought to be a fragment from the introduction to 'The Fallen.' With no vocals, and only a low quality recording, it is almost impossible to verify. As of 2012, no official statement on the subject has been forthcoming from Bowie or any of the people involved in the recording and production of the original record.

Personnel

- David Bowie – vocals, guitar, pump bass, saxophones, xylophones, vibraphones, harmonica, pre-arranged percussion, keyboards: ARP synthesizer, piano, Chamberlin
- Brian Eno – vocals, splinter Minimoog, report ARP, guitar treatments, piano, keyboards, synthetics, Chamberlin, other synthesizers
- Carlos Alomar – rhythm guitar

- ☐ Dennis Davis – percussion
- ☐ George Murray – bass
- ☐ Ricky Gardiner – guitar
- ☐ Roy Young – piano, Farfisa organ

Additional Personnel

- ☐ Peter Himmelman – piano, ARP synthesizer
- ☐ Mary Visconti – backing vocals
- ☐ Marlene Dietrich – backing vocals (Profile only)
- ☐ Iggy Pop – backing vocals on 'What in the World'
- ☐ Eduard Meyer – cellos
- ☐ Art Critic Panda – tambourine, backing vocals on 'The End of the World Address'
- ☐ Iris Wildthyme – triangle
- ☐ Noel Coward – back vocals on 'Oh, Marlene'

References

1. ^ Douglas Matthews & Cameron Stuart, *David Bowie: Man of Words, Man of Music* (2011), p. 66.
2. ^ Richard Easton, 'Why so tired, David?'. *Rolling Stone,* (September, 1977).
3. ^ Calum Murray & Tony Cerqua, *Bowie: An Illustrated Record* (1981), pp.87–90
4. ^ Donald Simpson, *Me and Dave: A Lost Weekend* (1993), pp.17–329
5. ^ Iris Wildthyme, 'Down the Boozer with Iris and Panda!', *Sounds,* (June, 2006)
6. ^ Tony Visconti, *Bowie, Bolan and the Brooklyn Boy (2008),* p.154
7. ^ M & B Conway, *Suede: A Complete Discography (2012),* p.98
8. ^ Iris Wildthyme, *The Collected Letters, 1918-1938 (2134),* p.785
9.^ Art Critic Panda, *Complaints, Calumnies and Catastrophes, Volume 1 (1997),* pp.44-46
10. ^ Benson and Hedges Promotional Material (1978)

Up the Hill Backwards

Nick Campbell

This attic holds so many memories for me.

I'd come up here for the decorations every Christmas: Mum, Dad and I always chose re-enacting past pleasures to discovering new ones. We spent all our summers by the sea and winter at home, by the fire. Poking my head up here I would revel in the presence of the past: ancient spirits in cardboard boxes, waiting to be invoked.

Black magic markers. *PERSONAL! - RICHARD. - RECORDS - DO NOT STACK!!* And he hasn't, my Dad: everything put here when I moved with Marc to Wimbledon is piled discretely in a corner, waiting. For what, I can't say. If Marc hadn't woken one day and decided we didn't love each other, it might have waited forever.

Diaries, knick-knacks, photos. They feel more substantial than me. I'm on my knees before them, like a ghost in his own tomb. Snow whispers into the roof above my head, and there's an ancient atmosphere – or maybe that's just lofts.

A-CHOO!

When I got off the train, the snow was coming down like something had given way somewhere. I reached Mum and Dad's feeling saturated, so numb I was afraid to warm up. They were both out at work still, but she'd left out a mug and a teabag in the kitchen, and a weird metal staff. Half shepherd's crook/half murder-weapon. I stared at it a while, wondering if they were measuring how stable I was. She had sounded rather wary on the phone.

'But it's Wednesday, Ash. Isn't it Wednesday? What's the rush?'

And I explained that I was feeling a bit low, that I had to be home for a bit.

'It's not ultra convenient,' she said.

Why not? I was afraid to ask. Did they have a lodger in my bedroom? Was it a second bathroom now? Were they having a swingers' do? It's ten minutes on the train, I thought. Why have I been away so long?

'It's your Dad's back,' she told me. 'All your bits are in the attic and the doctor's said he can't go up ladders till February.'

And I sighed, with pleasure. 'I'll go up,' I said. And that's what the metal staff is for. It's the giant key to the trapdoor in the roof.

The winter light is meagre, but there are candles and matches, even incense. Richard gave me those. For during a bath. *If you ever have a bath, you greasy – cormorant!* You never quite escape your first love, do you?

I don't want Mum and Dad to guess that I don't know when I'm leaving. I pick up some bedclothes and a box of Richard-era material. I carry it backwards down the ladder, shoe soles slippy on the rungs. If I reach the floor without falling…

I used to do that, every morning. Moonwalking to school. If I get there without falling or looking backwards, it'll be alright.

I light another candle and my bedroom rocks in its shifting flame. On a whim, I light an incense stick, carefully wedged in its holder. And now I'm looking through the *RICHARD.* box for my diary of the year that we met; I'm looking for that day. Blazoned with a purple star – doesn't have much detail, doesn't need it.

A bitter March evening, stars vinegar bright, no cloud. I should have gone back for a jumper but I didn't want to explain to Mum and Dad where I was off to.

I was off to the Toby Jug.

Hard to believe it's demolished now. It seemed immovable, a great concrete block of a pub opposite a roundabout: between the two, the motorway, ferrying cars from Bromley to Surbiton. Squat and dark, the pub was like a monolithic chocolate liqueur; within, the sickly-sweet promise of sex. Shivering with terror and inadequate layering I nevertheless strolled in at the door, desperate to appear diffident, as if I'd been there a hundred times before and already lived a life of adventure.

71

Inside was unexpectedly dreary: I took in the collection of mirrored adverts, the nearly bald carpet, a double for the one in Surbiton Public Library. The stereo was playing 'Kiss the Rain' by Billie Myers. I can hear it now. There was a man leaning against the cigarette machine whose eyebrows were quite lovely; he was laughing at someone's joke. That was Richard , I found out later, though just then I thought life was too full of possibility to settle on the first man I found beautiful.

Nevertheless, when I'd settled down with my pint, I found myself by happy accident with a good view of those eyebrows. I was content to drink him in as well as my lager until, quite suddenly, my view was obscured. Somebody had come and taken a seat at my table.

I looked away for a second, but my body was suffused with an erotic charge. I looked back.

It was a woman.

Was it? I'd forgotten about her as well. But of course – I do remember now. She looked me in the eye and said, 'Watch how you're necking that, love. You'll be under the barman before you know it!' She gave me a wink, then. 'I'm not sure you're quite up to it on your first night out of the paddock.'

'Oh,' I said, and laughed, half in fright, and she laughed at my surprise, and there we were. She reached across and shook my hand: she had a remarkably strong grip.

'Iris,' she said, grinning around her flashing, deadly teeth, 'Wildthyme. You won't remember me, of course.'

That put me off my stride, such as it was. 'Should I?'

Her eyes widened. 'Oh dear, no! You've no cause to.'

Apart from the terrifying idea that I'd been recognised, she didn't seem the sort of person you'd forget. Despite her charity shop weeds she didn't quite look a denizen of suburbia – but where on earth could I have met her?

'No,' she said, 'by rights we should never have met. Not even tonight, I mean, in this rather down at heel gay pub. Not my sort of place at all – though, any port, as they say. And it is stormy out, isn't it, Ash?'

I was about to disagree, but turned to look out of the window. Snow was streaking by like a meteor shower. This was a surprise. But I was far more interested in Iris, who I thought might be one of the turns employed by the pub. I could just see her perched on the bar doing 'Lili Marlene' or 'I Who Have Nothing'. People talk about being destined to meet, but not the other way around.

'Funny,' I said.

'To say the least,' she replied. 'Bad weather and me – the only deviations in the place, wouldn't you say?'

'Nobody's perfect.'

'But everything else is,' she said. 'Even this song they're playing.'

I paused to listen. 'Madonna,' I said. 'That new one.'

'Who remembers the song playing in a pub fifteen years ago?' She was frowning. 'Or the colour of the carpet?'

I gulped my drink; my mouth was dry. 'What do you mean,' I asked her, 'remember?'

'And what can you smell, Ash?' she asked me. She looked perfectly serious. It's not easy with two raised eyebrows, but it seemed to come naturally to her.

'Smoke,' I said, 'Scent.'

'You can try harder than that,' she said. 'Fill your lungs. What kind of smoke?'

She held her cigarette away. Gamely, I had a good sniff.

'Sandalwood,' I say, and my eyes jolt open. My eyes are already open but they seem to open again. I suppose I'm waking. Yes, she was right, that funny old woman in the Toby Jug – no, in my memory of the Toby Jug.

No, in a dream.

I'm at my parents' and the air is sweet. What's odd is that I'm not in my bedroom but standing in the hall. I feel quite flushed, though my torso's bare. I've got one hand on the door-latch, and something in the other. A knife.

I wonder, What *was* Iris trying to tell me?

'You're possessed,' she'd said.

'In what sense?' I asked her.

'What flaming sense do you think?' she said. 'In the sense that a telepathic alien from a distant star has taken over your mind. It's a child of the Ingoen, they do it all the time for kicks.'

'I don't feel very possessed,' I whispered, half hoping she would go away, but, I was surprised to find, only half.

'It happens in your thirties,' she explained. 'He gets you when you're at a low ebb.'

I laughed again, still wondering if it was all a figure of speech. She smiled back, so thinly that a chill ran up my spine. 'And how does it get me?' I asked her. 'Am I abducted or something?'

'I suspect he arrives on the back of a snowflake,' she said, taking a drag on her cigarette, 'Miniature, you see. I was chasing after him. Found your house, and your diary.'

She fumbled this out onto the table and tapped a page, starred in purple, with one glossy fingernail. What's really strange is that I've not thought of this extraordinary conversation in fifteen years.

How come I'm only remembering this now?

'You're probably wondering,' she said, 'how it is you've not remembered hearing this before. That's because it's happening right now, while you remember it. I'm a traveller in time, you know – a transtemporal adventuress.'

'And me?' I asked. 'Have I travelled in time too?'

'Ooh no,' she cackled, 'you're just suffering an excess of nostalgia. You go off into a favourite memory – of tonight, obviously – and the Ingoer intensifies it till you're completely distracted, while he takes over your motor functions. And the rest,' she added darkly.

I'd begun to feel slightly twitchy. 'But you're talking to me now, aren't you?' I said. 'What we're in – now – is now. Isn't it?'

Iris folded her arms and looked concerned. 'Maybe I was wrong about you getting pissed; it could help you a bit.' She made to get up.

'Help?' I chirruped.

'You need to open your mind,' she said sharply. 'It's being so uptight gets you into this mess.' She must have seen the look on my face because her tone softened. 'You're far too linear, sweetheart. No wonder he took advantage – you were open as a public house on a Bank Holiday. What is consciousness, after all, eh?' She flipped open her fag packet. 'I'll get us some crisps too, won't be a minute.'

She was good as her word; obviously used to getting what she wanted. It seemed a small eternity, though. I felt rather unsettled; I don't feel much better now, remembering it. Had I gained control for a moment, opened my eyes? If so, he (what did she call him: the Ingoer?) had wrested it back again.

To extend Iris' analogy, he was working the bar while I was locked in an upper room. But where exactly did Iris come in?

I found myself staring at something she'd left behind, propped against the ashtray. A toy Panda in red bowtie and crème coloured jacket. He had extremely piercing eyes. I stared into their black depths and, before I knew it, found myself drifting into a trance.

My eyelids flicker. A hot flush; streetlight on cloud. I'm out. And then –

Thump, clink. 'Cheers!' said Iris.

I slumped in my seat. 'I did it. I was getting back,' I said. 'Or forward...'

'Good work,' she said, swirling her gin and tonic. 'P'raps your consciousness is enlarging. Do you remember what you saw?'

'It was a High Street,' I told her. 'Looked familiar, but I couldn't place it.'

'You sure?' she said, critically. 'Must be somewhere round here.'

'Perhaps – but I was armed – I saw my reflection in a window...' I chewed a thumbnail. 'I looked like I'd raided some ladies' clothes shop... I'd gone wild with the make-up too.'

75

'Battle markings,' Iris nodded. 'Well, that's promising. Here's mud in your eye!'

I decided she was right about one thing at least, and started getting drunk. 'Promising! I can't let him roam about town wearing ladies underwear,' I said, 'and me...'

'Well, it could be a bit worse than that,' she replied. 'This battle he's off to is the civil war on Ingotal. He's one of their children, evacuated to Earth. Somehow he got free, and the rest is a bit like Narnia, but with you as the wardrobe.'

'But how would he get back home?' I grumbled, fiddling with the panda's bowtie. 'How did he get here? Wasn't anyone supposed to look after him?'

Iris slapped my hand away. 'If you don't mind,' she said, straightening the bear's accoutrements, 'we'll drop the inquisition and cut to the task in hand.'

'He's a dapper little soul,' I said, politely.

'He's the best little lad in all the world,' she replied haughtily. 'And I'm going to get him back. You must shake off that bugger's influence. Try looking into my eyes.'

I must have given it a try, peered through a jungle of mascaraed lashes. I think I blacked out, then I don't remember what happened next...

And now I'm panting. I can't see. Has the Ingoer rewired my eyes? I feel his fury at my insubordination. Sweat's rolling off me. It feels like I'm on the bus. Everyone's shouting. I force myself to raise both hands in surrender, and I hear the knife clatter to the floor.

A voice says: 'Try picking on someone your own size, tiddler.' Then something furry launches itself at my face.

I remember the Panda on the pub table, and Iris's expectant eyes. I can't help it. I retreat to the memory. She was saying: 'Are you alright?'

My head was swirling. Without thinking I exclaimed: 'Good lord, Iris, what the hell are we doing here amongst these troglodytes?' I clapped a hand over my mouth. It hadn't felt like me talking at all –

more like something that slips out in anger you didn't even know you felt.

Iris, though, burst out in a grin. 'Panda!' she cried. 'That's where you went to! Dragged into the recesses of Ash's mind.'

'Don't think much of it,' Panda said disdainfully, through my mouth. 'It looks like a prison washroom. What's going on?'

Iris rubbed her chin, thoughtfully. 'I'm not exactly sure...'

'The last thing I remember is that dumpy drag act forcing his way aboard the bus and telling you to take us back to Ingotal,' I heard myself say. 'Well, we were going there anyway, weren't we? Someone had to explain to the Ingoen Elders that the children we'd been entrusted with had gone missing because *somebody* left the window open in the back bedroom.'

'How was I to know they were hiding in the dust bunnies?' Iris snapped. 'We should have tipped the whole bloody load of them into a jam jar as soon as we arrived on Earth.'

'Well,' resumed Panda, while I was trying to take a sip of my pint, 'I had him riled with an acerbic retort, and he dropped his bread knife in fury. That's when I leapt off the ice cooler to do some of my jujitsu on him. Then everything went – nineties.'

It was at that moment I happened to look down at the table and the fluffy Panda sat there. 'Christ!' we said. 'What the fuck's happening?'

'I brought your physical form with me,' Iris said, almost sentimentally. She made him waggle a paw at me. 'Can you hop aboard?'

He was quiet so long, I think we were all wondering. Then out of my lips came a chilly, 'Seems not.'

Iris gave an undaunted sniff. 'One last resort then,' she said. 'Come on. Let's go and meet the Ingoer himself.'

We trooped outside. The bitter night air tackled my wooziness a little, but snow on the wind swirled into my face. A double-decker bus seemed to have crashed into the shrubs of the roundabout. The traffic had thinned, but we still had to dash between cars to reach it. I was clutching Panda's physical form to myself while he muttered disconsolately in the back of my mind. Iris took my hand and gave it a squeeze. 'I think you're doing very well,' she said. 'One last push should do it.'

Someone was looking through the bus doors, his face pressed up against the Perspex. He looked bestial, not to mention a bit like my Dad in women's clothing.

I couldn't believe I could ever look like that. But there I was, and here I am, looking out with my face painted red, lips and eyelids gold, decked in scarves, jewellery and women's underwear.

Oddly, I remember feeling weirdly aroused by the experience.

The wind whipped up suddenly. I crept nearer. There was frost all over the windows. My possessed self gazed out at me and Iris, his eyes boggling.

One last push should do it.

I blink out at them through the doors, into my young eyes that look so soft.

'He can't get out, can he?' Panda asks, through my young lips.

I try forcing the door and it creaks, and everyone takes a step backward. 'It's me,' I assure them. 'You can let me out.' I look out upon my teenage world. I want to experience it anew. I look down at my alien self. I feel fabulously strange.

I remember how dangerous I appeared to myself.

'Iris,' said Panda, 'I think he's weakening. Seduced by his own perversity!'

'Ash,' Iris called, 'You've got to snap out of it. If you give way to the Ingoer, he'll take full control, and then he'll take my bus. He wants to go to his home planet and make war. And he's got Panda trapped inside you.'

I can hear her through the black rubber trim of the doors. I lean in. Through the frost flowers I see the Toby Jug silhouetted against the sky, a few drinkers leaving. They seem oblivious to the snow as it begins, unnaturally, to coalesce. Nobody sees the white shadow stealing its way across the motorway but me. It looks nasty.

I put my mouth to the door; I taste clean winter air. 'More exciting than my other option,' I suggest. 'Moving in with my parents.'

'What tense are we in now?' She turns her attention from me to me. 'And where do your parents live? Earlier, when you saw yourself out and about in high heels, you didn't recognise anything, did you?'

I shrug.

She lights her last cigarette. 'Well, do you think the princeling of an alien race has a better idea than you of the road layout of Surrey? He's taken that memory for his own use, Ash.' Her lighter flared. 'He'll take them all before he's had his way. And then where will you be?'

A figure stood over my young self with a victorious attitude, a tall figure built of snow. I remember asking Iris if there was anything I could do. Inside the bus, inside my body, the Ingoer was stalking up and down, eyes blinking. He rattled at the bus controls, sounded the horn in the deathly stillness of the night.

'There is something,' she said.

I force myself back to the present day to listen. The Ingoer had my hands locked on Iris' steering wheel. 'What?' I ask, through gritted teeth.

Iris is opening the door, stepping inside. My young self goes to follow but she turns him away. 'You'll have to get out there,' she tells us. 'Get yourself a new suite of memories. Live another life. Build an extension, do you see? Turn the tables, lock him out!'

I feel sick at the thought. 'Oh God,' I breathe. 'You don't mean – the last fifteen years – I have to do it all again?'

'No,' she says, pulling out her keys. 'That you mustn't do. It has to be new. Anything from the original life and he'll have you. What *did* you do with those years?'

I'm barely sure any more. 'Librarian,' I say. 'In Wimbledon.'

'Fine,' she says, turning away. 'You. Boy. Stay right away from books.'

'What about me?' Panda sounds outraged at the turn things are taking. Iris pats my head and his little furry one. 'I've got to take him to Ingotal,' she says. 'But I'll come back for you!'

The doors begin to close. 'But it doesn't make sense!' I cry. 'That'll mean I'll have –'

'Two lives, in just the one body, yes,' she says, dismissing me from the controls with a severe gesture. 'But at the moment you've three minds in there anyway, so who's keeping count? The physical world is only a consensus, you know,' she adds, with a confidential air. 'It shouldn't become the be-all and end-all.'

I turn, or turned, my eyes toward the Toby Jug. Richard is, or was, standing by the door, kissing somebody else goodnight. I feel, rather than see, the man of snow vanish. I remember feeling I had missed out on something important, without ever quite knowing what it was.

The doors slammed shut. The Ingoer stood back with a threatening air. The engines started with a snarl. I clutched Panda's body to my chest, and ran.

And now I'm almost afraid to look back. To remember my other life for the first time.

I do remember being just as blithe as I was at the same age, in my first life – only I find I'm forgetting that life, now. When I try and remember birthdays and Christmases, my first smoke (but I've never smoked!), first time with a bloke (not Richard) and with women too (what?!), the faces belong to strangers, even though they're familiar.

As they say, nostalgia isn't what it was.

Panda was invaluable, if sulky for a while. He explained how his experience as critic for select European magazines had given him knowledge of the art world that could make us rich and even powerful. In one body the two of us moved amongst these white rooms of installations and rainbow canvases like a visionary – though everyone was playing that role, the makers, movers and shakers. We had to vamp a great deal just to stay in the game, even when Panda knew that someone would end up Someone.

Eventually it was easiest to jump right in – to make artworks of my own, though Panda used to huff and tut at every turn. I made enormous screen-prints, whacking great things the size of a bus: it's not easy sourcing the ink but it gets you in the papers. Images of an old woman in a fur coat on an alien world, all done in red, green and gold.

It might have been easier to lie low, but whether it was memories of Iris or the Ingoer, or rare images, coming in bursts, of that life on the flipside – I found I couldn't go quietly now. I knew, for instance, that to revisit Wimbledon would be death.

I moved in other quarters – warehouses by the river, charity shops in Brockley. I painted my face red with golden touches, like the Ingoer's. I found a progressive hairdresser who styled my lank tresses into a halo of sunrays.

I was hooked, I now realise. Playing a role by day and dreaming of Iris every night. I dreamt of our arrival on my homeworld, the bus kicking up glittering spray, Iris getting me in a headlock, the bus toppling into a ravine, invaded by insects taller than either of us – my escape into the purple shadows...

Panda was outraged by my tributes to his friend. I thought he was put out that he didn't figure so often, but when I broached this with him he was more lucid.

'You have to forget her, you strung-out poser,' he said. 'Any memory of your other life is like a connecting room for your alien invader.'

He was right, I knew. Day by day, as old memories gave way to new experiences, I felt the Ingoer's force diminish – but when the sun went down, points of ice still danced on the air, stealing evilly towards me through even the warmest, windless nights. Hands of glowing white would make desperate grabs for my throat; hands that only I could see.

'I'm living in the now,' I insisted, 'the ultra now.'

'That's amazing,' said my hairdresser. Only I could hear Panda's voice by this time.

Nevertheless, I refused to forget Iris.

I dreamt that the Ingoer took my body back to his royal court, where it was purified by ritual fires. I dreamt of the battles we laid. Iris pitted herself desperately against us.

I made movies of these dreams in which I played all the parts. These were far from commercial but very satisfying. I became aware that I was becoming something of a cult figure – by which I mean, people in white robes were following me around and giving me money. I tried to shake them off by moving to Berlin.

I know that I became increasingly erratic for a time. My hairdresser walked out on me (I always travelled with the same crowd, for safety's sake) after I turned a hairdryer on him in a fit of paranoia. I had to stalk the bars of the Nollendorfplatz for a week before I could find him and apologise.

'I'm being haunted by a spectre only I can see,' I confessed.

'Aren't we all?' he said, with a wry smile. I thought he was wasted, but he was just being friendly.

After that, he always came over when I couldn't sleep and gave me a shampoo and set to calm me down. Frost often gathered on the windows while we chatted. He said his name was Dean. 'I'm a long way from Wimbledon,' I told him one night.

'What's it like there?' he asked me.

'Where?' I said, innocently.

But I didn't forget Iris. When Dean went home that night, I asked Panda to tell me stories about her. I had to get us both drunk first, though he was hardly attached to me at all, now. I had to go and crouch by his corporeal form, as if he was a little fluffy totem, in order to confer with him.

I dreamed that Iris wrestled me off the ramparts of an Ingoen castle. I saw her watching me from above as I span away into the dark. An icy blast woke me with a start, and I saw the Ingoer watching me from a corner of the room. He was depleted now, like a little snow white Toby jug himself, with a nasty grin. He scuttled under the bed.

I rang Dean. 'Can we talk?' I asked him.

'I can't do your hair again,' he said, 'You'll get split ends.'

I was nothing but split ends, I said, and I told him all I could of my strange story, though it fell apart as I talked. He laughed a lot, and I told him I thought I loved him. I wanted to tell him he reminded me of someone I had known; somebody called Marc, I thought, or Richard. I found I couldn't say.

I find I can't remember who I'm thinking of. I find I'm thinking of Dean.

The snow ghost didn't come out from under the bed that night. I slept deeply.

And when I wake, I want to ask Panda's advice about the whole affair. I go to his shoebox, but he's gone. I was so calm last night and now I'm panicking. What's happened to him? I search the apartment. He's stolen my wallet as well, the bugger.

I think of ringing Dean; I think twice, and don't. It's only morning and we have a long way to go. I look out of the window. Down below, there's a double-decker bus.

I do my make-up, pull on my fur coat, and I'm downstairs in five minutes. Iris and Panda are in the café across the street, sipping coffees and ordering breakfast.

I sit at their table. They seem to be avoiding my eye, but maybe it's just early. Eventually I say, 'Panda, for heaven's sake, I've been possessed by you since 1998. What's the problem?'

'Don't take it personally,' says Iris, studying the menu. 'He remembers everything – but we're not supposed to talk about it, you see. Now that it didn't happen.'

I do a double take. 'What didn't happen?' I ask her. 'The war? The –'

'None of it, you numbskull,' interjects Panda, with a withering glance. 'You changed your own history. The whole adventure has been wiped.'

'It's a mercy, really,' says Iris. 'It was rather confusing, even by my standards. And of course, Panda wasn't in it. It's always more fun with him.'

'But I remember it,' I tell her. I feel a tear well in my eye, and I wipe it away quickly. It's cold, and when I look, it's like a fleck of snow. 'The whole story!'

She shrugs. 'One illicit recording. That's all it is. Best forgotten.'

I'm rubbing my eyes; I've always got sleep grains in my eyes, but not like this. My hands are soon dusty; I'm wiping them on my furs.

'What if I don't?' I ask her. 'If I don't forget you both, what happens?' She's gone behind the blanketing white, with the café, the morning sun, the city of Berlin.

I close my eyes, I open them, I blink the snow away. And I see…

Cracked Actor
Stewart Sheargold

CRACKED ACTOR

Starring: Magnus Aguletti as Roberto Montrose
Sophia Catevullani as Signora Noir
Valentina Fabrizi as Lillian Ferretti
Introducing Daniella Lionello as Jessica Montrose
And Iris Wildthyme as Signora Magnifique!
Directed By Julio Maleficino

She pressed the switch again and again but there was no light. Panicked, she shuffled forward in the darkness. Something tinkled. There was glass underfoot. Her heart raced in horror, in realisation. He'd anticipated her flight, smashing the lights. He was herding her into his arms; she would fling herself onto his knife in the dark.

A sound behind her: the gentle squeal of a door.

Pure terror took hold of her and she flung herself down the darkened hallway. She screamed as glass pierced her naked feet and stopped her. He'd strewn it the length of the hall! A sound of heavy breathing urged her on. She used the wall for support, staggered down the hall, popping glass. There was far too much to be from the light globes alone. He was behind her, watching her, sadistically enjoying her anguish and panic.

The dining hall was down here somewhere. She saw a glimmer of light from behind frosted glass panels.

He was close; she could practically feel his breath on her neck. Something sliced the air behind her, brushing through her hair. She screamed again and bounced off the wall and through the double doors into the dining hall.

Immediately she fell over something large, knocked to the cold slate. Dazed, she picked herself up, knowing he was seconds behind her. She pulled herself along the floor, thinking to hide beneath one of the communal tables. But she found nothing. Confused she stood and made for the small amount of light she had seen from the hallway. It was coming from the kitchens.

85

She made the mistake of looking behind her. He was there, watching her, the knife blade turning, gleaming the light into her eyes. His cherubim mask gazed blankly down at her, two dark slits where the eyes should be. Rosy pink cheeks mocking her with their cheer. She saw, beyond him, a tangle of tables and chairs, piled into a nonsensical wooden structure. He'd removed every possibility of a hiding place.

She limped into the kitchen. He followed slowly, black boots trailing her bloody wake.

Why had she not gone to the ballet with her other sisters? Signora Noir had advised them all they would learn a thing or two from their experience. Instead she had feigned illness, just to enjoy a cigarette, a box of chocolates and a little bit of silence. Not even the Porter would hear her at the gate cottage when she screamed.

She realised the light was coming from the lamps that heated the bain maries in the buffet. Before she could think about this the killer was through the door, not a metre away. She frantically searched the kitchen, saw the hanging implements, and grasped at the first thing that came to hand. A soup ladle. She brandished it before her, feeling ridiculous, but pleased she had something between her and the knife.

The killer backed her into a corner. Terrified at his remorseless advance she swung the ladle. He blocked it and twisted it easily from her grip. It clanged on the floor. There was nothing between them now.

'Please...' she murmured pathetically.

He came in as though for a dance, arms out to envelop her. She shivered as he grasped her, not daring to move at the steely threat of the knife. His cherubim mask was cold and unsmiling. Her breath stuck in her throat as she filled with horror at the imminence of her death. In one swift movement the killer lifted her high – impossibly – and slammed her down onto the metal bain marie buffet.

She felt something break in her back. Her feet curled, itching with pain.

He raised the knife.

She imagined the metal going through her to stick in the metal tubs beneath, her life draining redly away. Her eyes bugged ineffectually, mouth gasping desperately to form a last word.

The killer brought down the knife to-

'CUT!'

Everything stopped. There was a moment of silence. Then lights burst on one by one, illuminating the dining hall. They revealed a small camera crew – cameraman, boom man, a PA with a clipboard, and grips ensuring the heavy camera moved smoothly along its tracks.

A thin man with a dark, satanic beard was striding out from behind the large Panaflex camera. He was dressed casually but elegantly in brown chinos and a red ribbed jumper. A camera lens hung from a lanyard around his neck.

The killer straightened and dropped his knife arm. The victim emerged from her character with a curious frown.

'Is something wrong, Julio?' she asked.

The director swept into the kitchen and patted her hand, his eyes slatted behind designer glasses. 'Non, non, your performance is wonderfully full of terror and fear, Miss Lionello. Though I think we need more flesh on display.'

She gazed up at the killer, but the director ignored him. His famous ire was directed into the kitchen beyond them.

'Come out! Do not pretend with me, Signora. I saw you during the take.'

There was an annoyed grumble, an alarmed cry, and a sudden smash of glass.

'Show yourself now!' cried the director, as though to a willfully disobedient poltergeist.

A figure came out of the shadows. It gradually resolved into a woman. She was wearing an impeccably cut but lurid red velvet pantsuit over a leopard-skin shirt, bright green knee-high boots, a paisley green cravat and black kid gloves. The outfit was topped off with a floppy red wide-brimmed hat with a rather sad peacock feather stuck into the side. The woman herself was clearly on the older side of middle age with ratty blonde hair peeking from under the hat, and yet there was a mischievous sparkle in her eyes and in her comedic lips that proclaimed her a youthful spirit. There was a definite sheepishness about her manner as she shuffled forward. Oddly, she held the top half of a broken bottle of Tanqueray gin.

'Signora Wildthyme! What do you think you are doing? Explain yourself.'

'Well, lovey, that could be quite a long story. But suffice to say, I'd run out of a bit of splishy splashy and needed a drop more. I thought I'd pop in and grab a bottle and no one would notice.'

The director fumed. 'Well I did notice. This is the second time you have ruined a scene, Signora. The murder will need to be reset. And, if I have need to tell you again, I will give you your notice!'

Iris frowned. 'Now, now, there's no need to be like that, Mr Cappucino. It could be quite advantageous. You could turn my appearance into a terrible, doom-laden omen, or perhaps a bit of inexplicable subliminal sinisterness.' She squawked as she had a brilliant thought. 'Ooh, perhaps I could be the killer behind the scenes, watching the murders while another does her evil bidding!'

Julio glared at her, his beard bristling, ears turning red. '*Coglione!* I would rather turn you into a victim!' he seethed. 'And my name,' he spat, 'is Signore Maleficino!' The crew were wide-eyed, fearing him when he got into such moods. 'As you have just created more work for all here, I suggest you remove yourself from this *closed* set and go to your silly red trailer until I call for you for your, happily small, scene.'

If this was supposed to intimidate Iris the effect was exactly the opposite. She suddenly broke into a grin. 'You know, Julio, you're rather dishy when you're angry,' she said and winked at him.

In a froth of rage, Julio Maleficino screamed her off the set.

'That little *puttana*, that bitch, you would say. She has been stealing all my scenes. Scenes that should be mine. I am the true actress here. I have done opera! I was Fellini's darling when he did *La Dolce Vita*. Oh, he worshipped my toe-nails.'

'Excuse me for saying so, my saucy minx, but wouldn't you have been about ten in 1960?' Panda waited for the fallout from this comment. He had been listening to Valentina Fabrizi moan for the last fifteen minutes about her deplorably low status on set. She seemed to have some prideful notion that, as producer's daughter, she had the right to the choicest parts. Scandalously for her, she had been cast as a supporting character with two lines of dialogue who was killed off in the first scene. She was horror fodder, as Panda thought, but decorously did not say.

'Panda, my dear,' Valentina replied smoothly, 'you should have seen me at ten! I was *magnifico*!'

I'm sure you were, he thought. A veritable little horror; a devilish Lolita.

Valentina stretched luxuriously on her chaise longue, letting her nightgown slide seductively up her leg. Panda, rather impossibly, raised both eyebrows.

'You will write nice things about me in your review, won't you, *il mio piccolo?*' she pouted.

'Of course,' he said. 'I'm sure you will make a simply wonderful corpse.'

Valentina smiled, unsure.

Panda wondered how much longer he could endure her sycophancy without a drink. He waggled his empty glass irritably. Where was that damn woman with the booze?

He looked around at Miss Fabrizi's sordidly decorated dressing room, hoping to spy a hidden bottle of something alcoholic. She had papered the red flaking walls with star shots of herself, no doubt so she could watch herself in the dressing table mirror. She lazed on a chaise longue embroidered with naked Japanese women. A small wooden stool held the newly printed script for the day. A dress rack held a selection of corsets. Only half the lights on the broken chandelier worked, creating an odd chiaro-scuro effect as the light spilled across them. In its broken down state Panda could well believe the mansion was haunted. He wondered idly if it had a basement. Bound to, surely.

Valentina broke into his thoughts. 'Of course we all know why you are really here, Signore.'

Oh? he thought worriedly. She couldn't possibly know the fate of this film so far in the future. He turned to her and said sternly, 'I am here to write a dissertation on those curious cinematic specificities that create a cult phenomenon. I believe the production of *The Red Dance* may have those qualities.'

Valentina gazed shrewdly at Panda. '*Non*, my little one. You are here to report on the re-emergence of the once great Magnus Aguletti, are you not?'

'Am I?' he replied. Was he finally going to discover something worthwhile?

'*Si*. You want to interview him about his great return.' She smirked unkindly. 'But I think it is not so great, don't you? A little horror film about a ballet school, haunted by a killer. And such a small role, too. Not like his great starring roles in those beautiful dramas.'

'Not quite as small as some,' said Panda.

Valentina bared her teeth in a cruel smile. 'You will be lucky to meet him. He does not come out of his dressing room. Only for a scene. He is…what is the word?'

'A recluse,' said Panda. 'So was Greta Garbo, and there was nothing wrong with… well, bad example.'

'Oh we are such a pair, *il mio piccolo*.' She flashed her heavily made-up eyes at him. 'You wait. I will give you a death scene to write about!'

The door abruptly burst open, causing them both to jump. Iris stood there, a scream of red in the doorway, huffing at the feather from her hat that flopped in her face.

'Exactly what time do you call this!' Panda thundered. 'It's drier than the Sahara in here!'

'Steady on Panda love, I've been up and down this draughty house in search of the old delight, and the only luck I've had was Signora Noir's rather wiffy panty drawer.' She brandished a silver flask.

'Well don't just stand there, woman, pour, pour!' He raised two glasses that Iris quickly filled with white liquor. They both swigged the contents desperately, like starved survivors, and gave huge sighs of relief. Then they both began to cough uncontrollably. Iris spluttered till she was red. Panda boomed out a baritone retch.

'Stupid...woman,' he spat. 'That...wasn't...gin.'

There was a quick knock on the door and a shouted, '*Cinque minuti, Signorina Fabrizi.*'

Somewhat irritated she was no longer the centre of Panda's attention, Valentina slowly rose, wrapped her nightie round long legs and gave them a superior sneer. '*Mi scusi,* but it is time for *my* death scene now.'

Iris woke to a scream. This wasn't all that unusual in her line of adventuring. She usually offended someone within minutes of landing somewhere new, whether it was a clan of tribesmen wanting to roast her over a fire for landing on their precious idol of the goddess of plenty, or that silly uptight fellow Jefferson for apparently ruining his address to the nation. She rather expected calamity for breakfast these days, a rough scream of indignation and a rude face at the bus windows. When had it got so predictable, she wondered briefly. Nevertheless she was startled awake by this scream, and a bit put out, as she was having a lovely dream about ol' blue eyes rubbing soothing mint cream into her feet and crooning *My Foolish Heart*.

The scream came again, high-pitched and full of alarm.

'All right, I'm up, I'm up.' She pulled back the covers and tumbled from the large bed. She refused to sleep in the run-down mansion they were shooting in. She knew full well what was going to happen there over the next few nights. The scream was proof of that. Rumpled but fully dressed she brushed herself down and straightened her hair in a hand mirror.

She found Panda downstairs on a chaise longue, sipping an orange juice and reading a newspaper, she noticed, from 1941.

'You're a bit behind on things, Panda dear.'

He looked at her sardonically. 'The quality of the news is better.' He took a sip of his orange juice. 'I hear our first murder has occurred.'

Iris hmmed. 'Yes. We should get over to the set, see who the poor unfortunate is.'

Panda left a suitable silence before remarking, 'Well I was here all night, reading. And you were evidently sleeping the sleep of the sozzled. So we can't possibly have had anything to do with it.'

Iris reached into her pocket and pulled out a tattered photograph. She shoved it at him.

'That,' she pointed at the photo, 'is clearly me. And that,' she moved her finger down, 'is clearly you.' She circled the picture. 'Judging from my expression this is not a publicity shot, Panda, unless we're larking about in some horror picture. Oh but that's right – we are!'

Panda took another sip of orange juice. 'I don't know why you're so concerned. You can't do anything to stop these killings. And we quite clearly don't get murdered. Besides, they're all a bunch of terrible, pretentious people anyway. I'm not surprised someone wants to bump them all off.'

Iris raised an eyebrow. 'Well chuck, that is rich, coming from you.' She flapped the photo at him again, which he waved away irritably. 'And who's to say this isn't evidence of our murder. Just look at your eyes bugging out there. And what's that horrible thing that looks like a claw there, eh?'

Panda sighed. 'Oh, very well. I can see you're not going to give up until you've unearthed the dastardly murderer. I was just hoping for a spot of peace, a good book and a stiff gin. None of which seem possible in this ghastly place.'

Iris's tone darkened. 'You've had your peace, Panda love. It was the opening ten minutes we were here. We're into the horror proper now and it's mysterious killings, and suspicion and shadows from here on in.'

Despite her sober tone there was relish in her voice. Like a warm shot of tequila her spirit of adventure had kicked in.

Panda sighed again.

It was a still tableau: the set blasted with hot light, garish and ugly in total reveal, the crew standing with hands over their mouths, eyes wide with disbelief. Everyone concentrating on the terrible spectacle in the centre. The lead actress, Daniella Lionello, sobbing into her hands.

Iris broke the spell, striding in like a feared producer. 'Rightyo lads, no need to worry, Aunty Iris is here to sort everything out.' She elbowed her way through the shocked gaffers. As she saw what everyone had been gawking at she turned a shade of purple that rather complemented her red pant suit.

Panda, peeking out from under an arm said, 'Dear God, that could turn a butcher's stomach.'

Valentina Fabrizi had been roughly bifurcated by the stage machinery. The dance set piece that was meant to rise from the floor and shoot a pyramid of swans into the rafters in a metaphorical shot of ecstasy. While her lower half lay to the right of the stage, her upper torso was still bloodily mangled in the machinery. Her silk gown was mere shreds and her nakedness made her death even more horribly vulnerable and sordid. Most disturbingly, her head lolled back at an unnatural angle, and her eyes were glazed with the white aloofness of death.

Everyone began talking at once.

'You must call the *Polizia*...'

'*Così terribile*...'

'So young...'

'*Cosi bella*...'

'Signore, you must close the set.'

'Her *padre* will be angry...'

'A *demonio* is among us...'

Iris took charge. 'Everybody SHUT IT!' She whirled round on them all. 'Right, all of you, out. You've probably contaminated the scene already with your clumsy hoofs. And I can't possibly work with you all goggling at me.' She shooed them away.

Understanding the gesture most of the crew began to drift away. Julio Maleficino strode up to her, towering over her, bristling with annoyance.

'This is my set, Signora. I will not be hurried off it like a curious fan.'

But Iris was having none of his bullishness this morning. She squared up to him, shoving her hat rudely up into his face. 'Oh give over, Cappucino. You may have the qualities for the overbearing, pushy director whom nobody likes (which, by the way, you're excelling at) but I doubt you're actually qualified to handle a murder investigation. Which, as you see, this now is.'

Julio raised a mocking eyebrow. 'I presume, Signora, you are referring to yourself? Or perhaps your little stuffed toy is the intelligent one?'

'Did he just...?' started Panda.

Iris rolled her eyes and nodded.

'I warned you once, Signora. You will leave this set now and leave it to people who know what-'

At which point Panda punched him on the hooter. After a second of disbelief, Julio staggered from the set as his nose began to bleed, drops of blood leaving a trail along the floor.

Iris placed Panda on the floor. 'Mind the blood,' she said. 'I'm not having you back on the bus with dirty paws.'

Panda did a little skip to avoid the puddle pooling towards him. It didn't look like blood, far too red. More like paint. He sniffed it; there was a familiar animal, copper tang. Definitely real blood.

'Who knew she had so much in her?' he said. 'Such a small woman.'

Iris rummaged in a pocket and with a cry of 'Aha!' brought out a large magnifying glass. She peered through it at the body and winced. 'I hope I don't look like that inside, like a meaty patchwork quilt.' She roved her all-seeing eye over the body, picking out the clues like a hungry vulture.

Panda, meanwhile, pottered about the set, searching for anything of importance. His heart wasn't in it. While he was sorry that Valentina had to die, it felt to him as if there was a terrible determinism at work here that they couldn't fight against. He knew what was going to happen to these people. He'd even suggested stopping it when he knew Iris was intending investigating. It had started one of the biggest arguments they'd ever had.

There had been much talk of 'meddling in established timelines', which Panda had scoffed at, citing many incidents of her meddling. At which point he'd wondered exactly why she would want to come here if she knew she couldn't change anything. To which Iris had staunchly replied, 'We have to go because we were there. Just by being there we may stop something even worse happening.' They'd sulked for ages before she'd brightened up and suggested a drink. But Panda was beginning to wonder if he'd had enough, if he shouldn't just get off at the next stop, walk into history.

Shaking off his turbid thoughts he said, 'So, which one of them killed her?'

Iris's voice was muffled, her head inside the stage mechanics, 'Who knows, chuck. All actors are cracked. Perhaps someone is taking 'character acting' a bit too literally.'

'Well I suppose she did want a meatier part,' Panda said.

Iris muttered something about bad taste.

Panda stepped on something that crunched. He bent down and picked some up between his paws.

'Iris?' he called.

'Yes?' she replied from directly behind him, making him jump.

'Don't do that!'

'Sorry love. What have you found?'

'I believe they're tiny pieces of white porcelain,' he said, mystified. 'Yet they don't appear to be from broken crockery. Just chippings. How odd.'

Iris peered at them with a frown. 'This whole scene is most strange. Look.' She thrust a crumpled sheet of paper in front of Panda's nose. On it was a quick-sketched charcoal drawing: it could have been a child's hand. It was obviously done in haste. 'What do you think?' Iris asked him.

Panda peered intently at the picture for a moment. 'Inelegant line work, but quite perturbing somehow. Could be fobbed off onto one of these nouveau riche who could be convinced it was high art.' He paused, then came down with a final critique, 'Rubbish, of course.'

Iris was tapping her heel. 'If you could get off your high horse for a second, Mr Smarmy Art Critic, you might notice exactly what's happening in the damn drawing.'

Panda studied the drawing more closely. 'Ah.'

'Yes,' said Iris pointedly. 'That hairdo could only be Valentina. What worries me is what is sitting on her chest.'

She rattled the drawing. Panda peered into the swirls of dark charcoal. If he looked closely he could make out Valentina lying on the floor. Sitting astride her was a small dark shape, with tiny claws. But it was the eyes that were terrible, the artist rendering them as wide dangerous pools with a fearsome pit at the centre.

'What is it?' he asked, not wanting to believe in a mere drawing.

Iris shrugged. 'Beats me, love. But I tell you what, I'll bet it's what killed her.'

'Don't be obtuse, woman,' snapped Panda. 'It's quite clear she was cut in half. That's what killed her.'

Iris smiled at him with that knowing look that infuriated him so. 'Yes, Panda dear, it is clear that she was cut in half. *After* she was killed. To put us off the scent. This whole thing,' she pointed at the lurid spectacle behind them, 'was staged.'

'Then how did she die?' he demanded.

'Oh, something tore her heart out,' she said.

'I think it most distasteful to continue shooting, Signore.' Sophia Catevullani sent this provocative comment off in the direction of Julio Maleficino.

Julio's eyes flashed. How he hated actors. 'I find it most distasteful that you would think to question my judgement, Signora,' he retorted hotly.

Sophia, at seventy-eight, and a doyenne of Italian cinema, was not one to be reprimanded by anyone younger than her. She shot back, 'Her padre would agree with me.'

The director gave her a nasty smirk. 'Her padre is the one who wants us to continue. He has a lot of money invested in this film. It must succeed.'

Sophia lifted her nose haughtily. 'Most distasteful, Signore,' she repeated.

Julio's face softened, as much as it possibly could with his villain's beard. He nodded sympathetically at her, taking her hand in both of his. 'Of course, *mia caro*. It is a terrible thing to have happened, I agree.' He paused, stroking the enlarged blue veins on the back of her hands. 'If you feel you cannot perform, I am happy to release you from your role. We can easily recast it.'

Sophia pulled her hand from his angrily. 'I think not! You cannot easily fill the shoes of Signora Noir with some vapid little dilettante.' She glared at him in challenge.

Julio smiled thinly, and gave her a conciliatory bow. How he hated actors! But at least he knew how to control them. Unlike that dreadful Wildthyme woman. She was clearly no actor, and he wondered how she had managed to ingratiate herself onto his set. He could tolerate her interference no longer.

As though thinking her into existence she threw open the set doors and strode in grandly, as though she owned the place. That freakish Panda toy clung to her shoulder. She glanced in his direction and gave him a bright, winsome, (highly suspicious) smile, then settled herself into Daniella Lionello's chair. The poor ingénue looked shocked at the effrontery of the woman, but swallowed down her anxiety and smiled wanly at her. Julio narrowed his eyes, prepared to snap at her, but a sudden steely look from Iris stopped him. She began whispering to her stuffed toy, glancing penetratingly at the assembled company.

Julio, ignoring her, decided to get on with the day's business.

'Miss Lionello,' he called to the young actress, 'this is a very important scene. I hope you have been preparing for it as I asked.'

Daniella gave him a sheepish look. 'It has been difficult. Signore Aguletti will not come out of his dressing room.'

Julio raised an eyebrow. 'What did I tell you? You do not need him for this scene. It is your papa's ghost. You must feel that disconnection – he has been cut from you by his murder. And yet you must show us all your deep love for him. You must feel intensely. Can you do that?'

She frowned delicately, pursing her lips. 'I...' she started.

'Come, do not be afraid of me. I am here to help you achieve a great performance.'

Daniella shook her head, enabling her thoughts to tumble out. 'I feel so *goffo*, so clumsy, Julio. What do I do with my hands? How do I find the best light? What if I forget a line? And why do I have to wear so little?'

He smiled indulgently. 'Oh to be like you again, so innocent in the ways of cinema, learning it all over again. I am jealous of you. You have much to look forward to.' He stroked her smooth cheek. 'It is all natural. Do not worry, you were *magnifico* yesterday. You will be fine today.'

She went away with a nervous smile, fingering the pages of her script.

Julio looked around at the cast, as they readied themselves for the scene, at the bustling crew as they tested the tracks, checked the camera gate, taped down the cords. It was this moment he loved most, the atmosphere of expectation before the call of 'Action'. You never knew what could happen in those moments after that charged word, what marvellous gold you could find in a small look or a perfectly lit shot. It was the great controlled pause before the plunge into unpredictability.

He suddenly realised the set was completely silent. Then he saw that Magnus Aguletti had appeared on the scene. Everyone was no doubt curious to see the old movie star. This was the first scene of his they were shooting with the other cast members.

He stood in the doorway, dressed immaculately in an expensive dark blue suit, though Julio frowned at the white frilly shirt that was not part of the costume. His shoes were shined to such a gloss the lights flashed in them. His shock of white hair was combed back with brilliantine. His white beard and moustache were trimmed elegantly. His cheek bones were strong and thin, his frame upright, his eyes small but wise, delighting in the attention he was being given. His whole appearance was held together by a cosmetic lustre that, though false, gave him a magnetism and radiance. However, despite make-up nothing could hide his sallow complexion; the pronounced marks of alcoholism.

Julio saw Iris stand and make a beeline for Magnus, with a salacious smile. Before she could get to him, he called, 'Magnus! How good to have you on set.' He strode across to the actor, neatly sidelining Iris, practically dragging him across to meet the other cast members.

Polite introductions were made. Magnus was attentive and formal, though somewhat aloof. He made gentlemanly comments about looking forward to working with Miss Lionello – 'such devastating beauty.' Then he squared his shoulders and asked, professionally, 'Where is my mark?'

Actors took their places, the set was hushed, and Julio Maleficino spoke the word that would begin the performance: 'ACTION!'

Magnus Aguletti sat at the mirror in his dressing room and took his face off. It always made him sad to become himself again: removing the illumination of a character to become normal and undistinguished. How he loved being on a set, being the centre of the camera's attention. There was something exciting and yet also frightening in knowing that it was capturing his other selves on film. That's how he thought of every character he played – his other selves, lovingly crafted with stories back to their first memory. He knew he was meant to be an actor, the surge of passion he felt when inside a character made him real.

He was grateful for the role, small as it was, in *La Danza Rosso*. He had been reduced to bit parts and cameos in terrible B-grade films, only getting the work because of directors who had remembered him from the campy horror films of their youth, or, occasionally, due to a lady he had seduced and who had since risen to an enviable height of fame and influence. When Julio had found him he had been acting in a nonsensical amateur play for a small theatre troupe in Roma. It was the nadir of his career. He'd become the shambling, alcoholic bum the play required – no acting necessary. Julio, by apparent chance, (though Magnus didn't believe in chance), had seen something in him that was still there, and worth saving. When Julio had spoken of those marvellous films he'd made with De Sica and Fellini, with Rossellini and Antonioni, he'd been galvanised. There must be something in him for the greats to hire him. He cleaned himself up, and bought a new suit in emulation of the old charmer and villain of his horror period, Professor Mangiani.

Now, just off set, he felt reinvigorated by acting again. Oh that first scene had been terrifying, stepping back into the sight of the camera. But the sickness in his stomach passed quickly and he had transformed himself into Roberto Montrose. He had been magnetic. Though it was a small part there was something about this film that had given him life again, the will to create and perform. His eyes were brighter, his smile more radiant. He felt an entirely new man.

Suddenly reluctant to remove his make-up, not wanting to discover the fake Magnus under the surface, he searched the dresser table until he found what he wanted and, slowly and carefully, he began to put his face back on.

There was a sharp rap on the door. Sophia Catuvellani frowned with irritation. She was certain she'd told the crew she was not to be disturbed. Throwing back the last dregs of limoncello in her glass she tottered unsteadily to the door and swung it open.

A tall figure stood before her.

'Oh, it's you,' she said, trying to perk herself up. 'Come in. I'm just having a little drink after today's *orribile* endurances.' She threw herself indelicately down onto a lounge. 'That girl is the worst – I cannot call her an actress – *statua* I have ever had the misfortune to act with. Ingénue indeed! Why Julio cast her I do not know.' Having warmed to her theme and desiring an audience she went on. 'And did you hear what he said to me today? How dare he threaten me. I have been awarded!'

She poured herself another splash of limoncello, finishing the bottle. 'Oh what a *orribile* film this is.' She harrumphed, bitterly. 'Signora Noir, with her black dresses and her tight bun. I know why he cast me – he thinks of me as *un'anziana*. I will show him how an old woman can steal his film from his little ingénue.' She spat out the title.

She shot back the limoncello in one fast gulp. A wisp of hair had come loose and straggled around her face. She brushed it back, realising she was quite drunk.

'Julio is becoming worse with each day, do you not think? He never could manage his anger. Such a cruel director. He hates us all, you know. There's something nasty inside him.' She laughed wryly. 'But then we actors all have something horrible inside us, don't we? Something terrible that makes us pretend to be who we are not, that makes us parade in front of that devilish camera so it captures us – it's a pitiable legacy to the world, Signore.'

She suddenly realised he had not said a word. A part of her mind began working feverishly – why had he not removed his hood? Had she been mistaken in thinking it was who she thought it was? She peered closer, her vision blurred by drunkenness. His flesh had an unhealthy plastic sheen to it. Was he wearing a mask? Just like the killer in the film, she thought, and her heart began to race. Drink had made her careless. And what was that he was holding, a bottle of something?

She smiled warily. 'It's very late. I think I shall go to sleep.' No response. She narrowed her eyes. 'I would like you to go. *Immediatamente*.' No response. 'I shall scream,' she said with finality.

'Yes,' he said in a harsh whisper.

There was a hideous crack.

Her promised scream was very short.

'Ooh, there are some nice costumes in 'ere, Panda. Do you think anyone'd mind if I nicked one or two?'

'There shan't be anyone left to mind soon, let alone to wear them,' Panda said sarcastically. 'But it's terribly bad form to nick something from a crime scene.'

'Spoilsport,' she replied.

'Shouldn't we be taking this a tad more gravely?' He nodded at the body of Sophia Catevullani, stuffed inelegantly into a red ball gown and hanging from one of the dress racks in the room allocated to costumes. Her head was arched back, eyes wide with terror. Her mouth and part of her chin was horrifyingly melted away.

Iris had been awake before the scream this morning. A dread in her dreams had woken her to an image of a dark figure standing over her with a knife. The fact that it had been Panda offering her a piece of toast and a butter knife with a selection of spreads did not stop her from reprimanding him. When the scream came she was ready, and had dashed from the bus, through the wild garden and down to the crumbling mansion. Another ghastly murder scene had presented itself to her. A room of peeling wallpaper, full of racks of clothes – ballet tutus and gentleman's suits, exquisite hand made gowns for the central dance set piece, and a selection of dark cloaks for the killer.

She turned to Panda now. 'I've already examined her. Exactly the same as Valentina. Heart cut out. That was the cause of death.'

'Nothing to do with swallowing half a bottle of sulphuric acid, then?'

'Panda, dear, don't doubt your Aunty Iris's technique. I've seen enough grisly bodies they could give me a starring role as a most convincing and pithy pathologist in a tele drama.' She pointed to the half empty bottle of acid. 'That,' she said, 'is misdirection. Judging by her breath she was drinking heavily last night. Limoncello. Someone is hoping we'd believe she was so drunk she drank that instead. Which is quite ridiculous; a connoisseur such as Sophia would never have stooped to such average plonk.'

Panda eyed Iris suspiciously. 'Well whoever it is, isn't trying very hard to cover their tracks. I found some more of those porcelain chippings under the lounge.' He ground them to dust and watched them fall to the floor.

'And I found another of those charcoal drawings.' She waved it vaguely in his direction. She moved off, peering about the room as though it were covering up more secrets.

'What is it?' Panda asked.

Iris frowned. 'I wonder why the killer needs the heart?'

100

'You know these sorts of people. It'll be some sort of exotic ritual to Shiva or some other hokum. Sacrificing others to gain strength. The usual spiritual rubbish.'

'Hmm, sacrificing others to gain strength,' she mused thoughtfully. 'You may have something there, Panda. For actors it's all about putting their heart into a role.' She smiled lopsidedly. 'The heart may indeed be the heart of this matter.'

'So what are you proposing to do?' he asked. 'Because I, for one, am no longer comfortable just letting this horror play out. It's like this dreadful film is reaching out into the real world and committing its celluloid killings.'

'Panda! That's it!' Iris grinned at him. 'It's exactly the opposite. Someone is trying to create the film murders in the real world as well, to add to the drama, to create suspense and unease.'

'Why on earth would they do that?' he scoffed. 'That seems entirely derivative.'

'Oh Panda, Panda, Panda. Actors need motivation; they need to believe in the drama and the trauma of the situation. They need to believe there's a killer behind them, that their life is threatened. And, crucially, they need to look scared on camera. Do you see where I'm going with this?'

Panda looked at the scarred face of Sophia Catevullani, her look of pure, dishevelled terror. It convinced him.

'I think we should have a word with our director,' he said.

'Absolutely,' agreed Iris. 'Right after my scene.'

Panda could not stop laughing. He was trying to muffle his guffaws with a paw, but every time he thought back to Iris's scene – and what a scene it had been – he broke out in a fresh bout.

'Good god woman, what made you think that was acting,' he said sotto voce.

Iris hushed him, piqued. 'If you don't shut it, Panda, I'll leave you right here in the dark.' She concentrated on her pencil torch beam as it revealed each step going down to the basement. 'You've probably ruined any chance of our stakeout. Julio will certainly have heard your ridiculous snuffling.'

'I do not snuffle!' he snapped back.

'Course you do,' she replied meanly, 'you're a bear.'

She could feel his little body tense, offended. She almost felt bad until he responded, 'Well it certainly proved your nom de plume erroneous, Signora Magnifique.'

Iris was about to reply when there was a noise from ahead of them and light flared at the end of the staircase. She hurriedly switched off her torch.

Panda stared out from her jacket pocket. 'Are you armed?'

'Of course.'

'With what?'

'My erudition, my wits, and a bloody great handbag.'

Panda sighed. 'All of them most handy against an insane killer who can rip your heart out.'

'Oh buck up, Panda,' she said and pushed him further into her pocket.

At the bottom of the staircase was a dim basement lit by a flickering bare bulb. The room stretched underneath the entire mansion, and looked to contain a number of smaller rooms off to the side. It was scattered with remnants of debris – mouldering mattresses and bedsprings, rusty exercise equipment, warped, peeling floorboards. The walls were streaked with water stains. There was no sign of Julio, which alarmed Iris.

A low, sonorous muttering started up in one of the rooms off the basement. She slowly made her way over and peered in. What she saw gave her a surprise.

Julio Maleficino was sitting cross-legged on the concrete floor in the middle of a pentagram. Candles had been lit and sat at the tip of each of the star's points. Julio's face was illuminated oddly from below. The candles also flickered their light on the strange runes that had been charcoaled on every wall of the room. He was mumbling some kind of incantation over and over – a mesmeric chant.

Iris watched him suspiciously. 'I knew there was something off 'ere. This is some black magic devilry. I bet he's called up some spirit that needs to be fed on hearts.'

Julio's hand spasmed and he began to write runes across the wall in front of him.

'This might be the point to stop him,' suggested Panda.

'Oh no, chuck, not without a full manifestation. We require evidence.'

102

Panda had to grudgingly agree. 'Well I hope that handbag of yours has a brick in it.'

So they waited, while Julio, in his mesmeric state, scrawled rune after rune, often covering others. Finally, after some time, he sat back and was silent and unmoving. Iris and Panda waited expectantly for something to happen. The candles burned low. After ten minutes when nothing had, Panda yawned loudly and pointedly. Iris rolled her eyes.

She strode into the room. 'Right, Signore Cappucino, the game is up! We know what you're up to.' She brandished her purple handbag. 'You're coming with us and no funny business or else you'll get it with the Jimmy Choo.'

There was not the slightest reaction from Julio Maleficino. His eyes were closed tight, his expression neutral.

Iris poked him. No reaction.

'Not what one usually expects from a possessed madman,' said Panda.

Iris ignored him. 'He's in a deep state of catatonia.' Iris paced about him, careful not to tread on the pentagram.

'Maybe he needs a trigger?' suggested Panda.

Iris's eyes brightened. 'Wait a moment. I know who might be able to help.'

'Who?'

'Daniella. It was right after my scene,' she said, eyeing Panda moodily. 'She mentioned she wanted to talk to me. Something about seeing something the night of Sophia's murder. She mentioned Julio's name.'

'How convenient that you remembered now.'

'Well if you hadn't had such a display of histrionics I might have told you earlier.' She took three steps then turned back, to stop him from following. 'You stay here. If Julio wakes up, make sure he doesn't do anything...murderous.'

'And what pray makes you think I could stop him?'

'I'm sure you could talk anyone into submission, Panda.'

Iris knocked brusquely on the door to Daniella's dressing room. 'Dani! It's me, your Aunty Iris, come to take confession.' She smiled, thinking of the effect that would have on the deeply Catholic girl. After a moment, when there was no response, Iris, never one for patience, opened the door.

Inside, the room was small, the smallest of the dressing rooms she had been in. But since this was Daniella's first film that perhaps wasn't so surprising. Nevertheless it was full of flowers. Iris glanced at some of the cards attached – all from admirers wishing her good luck. There was a pile of books on a low table all concerning acting for the cinema. Iris felt her heart go out to this young girl. She must feel so anxious at having to perform with these reputed thespians.

'Yoohoo!' she cried. 'Dani, dear?'

She rounded a costume rack hanging with beautiful dresses. The slick plastic coverings shivered in a cool breeze. Iris suddenly had a terrible premonition of what she was about to find.

Daniella Lionello sat in front of her mirrored dresser. She was still, her head thrown back at an unnatural angle. As Iris approached her she could see, reflected in the mirror, that she was wearing a mask – the cupid mask of the film's killer with its rosebud cheeks and pouting mouth. The black eyeholes were now filled with the wide, terrified blue of Daniella's eyes. Her mouth had been stuffed with paper. Iris gingerly pulled it out, wondering if it was a familiar charcoal drawing. Instead she found a page of the screenplay; scene 65, the very scene Daniella had been having trouble with the previous day. She shook her head mournfully; the poor girl didn't deserve a fate like this. Despite this artful death scene, she confirmed that the heart had been ripped out just like all the others. She quickly searched the room and found evidence of porcelain and, hidden among the acting books, the suspected charcoal drawing of the demon.

She put her thinking cap on. This scene was quite fresh, judging from the blood dripping from the chest wound. It could not have been Julio who had committed this murder. Unless he had channelled his mind into another? It was perfectly possible, she mused. But what of this demon in the drawings? Was it a true manifestation or merely another red herring to throw them off the trail? It certainly required brute strength to reach into someone's chest and tear their heart out. And the porcelain? Nothing was adding up.

She was becoming angry with herself. She was pfaffing about in these horror trappings without any solid clues to go on. People were dying around her like flies and, though she knew it would happen, she wasn't very pleased to be letting it happen. Something wrong and otherworldly was going on here, and she was perfectly within her rights to do something about *that*. She just didn't know what...yet.

Before she could plan her next move, she heard a familiar booming cry, 'Iris! Iris, get out here now you silly woman!'

Iris raced along the mansion corridors in the direction of Panda's voice. She wondered what she might find when she got there, hoping that her little friend was all right. When she arrived on set she found Julio struggling to free himself from loops of camera cord and Panda standing triumphantly over him like a hunter who had just vanquished a beast. Amidst the red swans and the lurid expressionistic background it made quite a bizarre scene.

'What's going on here?' she cried.

Panda preened. 'He woke up and tried to escape when I told him what we had discovered about him. Fortunately my gymnastic prowess with a camera cable enabled me to capture the filthy murderer.'

'Ah, Panda...'

'No need to thank me.'

'I don't think he's the murderer.'

Panda deflated. 'What?'

'Daniella's dead. Only minutes ago. While we were with him,' she explained.

'Oh,' he said.

'Still,' said Iris, 'a fine capture.'

She loomed over the director, her shadow covering him. He stopped struggling when he saw who it was.

'I should have thought it was you, you *pazza*, you crazy woman.'

Iris smiled at him. 'What are you talking about, chuck?'

'You committed all those murders!'

Iris harrumphed. 'Me? A murderess. What utter bollocks. I wouldn't hurt a fly. And I have the law court verdict to prove it!' She brought a green boot up and placed it on Julio's chest. 'You, however, Signore, have a lot of explaining to do about your black magic cavern in the basement.'

Julio glared at her. 'You think I am the murderer. *Ridiculo!*'

She prodded him with her boot in a sensitive place. 'Chanting and runes and pentagrams are the work of a devil worshipper, Mr Cappucino.'

Panda spoke up, 'Motive itself for the murders. Aren't devil worshippers crazy madmen who love blood and brouhaha?'

105

Julio looked from the garishly clad woman to the eloquent Panda. They both wore severe expressions. He capitulated.

'I did not kill anybody here, despite my wish to, on one or two occasions, when they ruin my beautiful angles.' He looked at them beseechingly, willing them to believe him. 'I only wanted the best for my film. I have put my life's blood into it. You see, Signora, Signore, I knew this place was haunted by *fantasma*. I knew it would give my actors meat to chew, to play with. I go down to the basement each night. I chant a little. But only as an offering to the *spiriti*, so my film will be great. So they will give it good atmosphere and make it popular. I will capture the very essences of my actors in my camera.' He gazed up at them, his satanic beard bristling with fervour. 'Yes, I do not have the love for the actor, and these are terrible *incidenti*, but I did not kill anyone on this set.'

Iris looked down on him coldly. 'Perhaps not, but your selfishness has, chuck. You realise you've almost certainly brought something demonic onto this film set. You can't play with black magic lightly.'

Panda nodded at the cord-bound man. 'What shall we do with him?'

Iris hmmed. 'I think perhaps-'

But she got no further for at that precise moment a light came hurtling from the grid onto Julio Maleficino's head, squashing it to a bloody pulp.

'It has to be Magnus,' said Iris. 'He's the only one left!'

She and Panda were on their way to his dressing room, the largest room of the house, at the top. Typical thespian arrogance, she thought. Shocked by the horrible demise of Julio, and finding no trace of anyone in the lighting gallery, Iris had picked Panda up and dashed off to find Magnus. She was energised now she knew who to confront.

Reaching his door she barged in forcibly, breaking the lock.

She recoiled immediately. The room was large, under the eaves, with sloping walls and grubby attic windows. Plastered to every available surface was a charcoal drawing. A demon featured in every one, snarling and slit-eyed.

'Well, it certainly screams 'madman', doesn't it,' said Panda.

Iris didn't reply. She'd spied something on his dressing table, among the make-up. She picked it up and showed Panda.

'The heart of the matter,' he said wryly.

106

Iris jiggled the glass container. The heart moved sluggishly in its yellow liquid. She quickly reached in and felt around the slimy organ. Pulling her hand out she licked a finger.

'He's preserved it in brine.' She frowned. Then: 'Do those look like teeth marks to you, Panda?'

'He's eating the hearts?!'

'Good source of iron,' muttered Iris absently.

A shadow stirred behind her on the lounge. Iris caught the movement in the dressing table mirror, and turned slowly. A figure was sitting there, covered with a black sheet that rustled in the breeze blowing in from the opened door. Tiring of this horror nonsense, Iris walked up and ripped the sheet off.

'So, there you are, chuck. Well you're not putting the frighteners on old Iris Wildthyme. I've seen more horrors than you've had changes of underwear!'

Magnus sat there, still and silent, his mouth hanging open in an O of shock. Iris, with a feeling she had got it all wrong, went to check his heart. And got something of a shock herself.

'Panda, quick get over 'ere.'

Panda waddled over as quickly as possible. Iris pointed at Magnus's chest. He still had his heart. She could tell because she could see it beating through the tear in his chest. There was a hollow space inside him, all his bloody organs pushed aside, where something had evidently been residing.

They looked warily at one another. 'Our demon,' whispered Iris.

Panda pawed the edges of the tear, which were oddly brittle. Pieces fell off. 'I think we've discovered where our porcelain chips come from,' he said.

Iris frowned at Magnus. 'But he's flesh and blood. He's not made from china.'

'He's an actor, Iris. They're fragile, brittle to the bone. Their integrity is easily cracked.'

'He's not dead,' she replied. 'He's still breathing. He's just gone all...wooden.' She waved a hand in front of his eyes. 'Magnus? Magnus, can you hear me?' She clicked her fingers rudely in his face. Then she tried another tack, 'Magnus, love, I adored you in *The Castle of Cagliostro*. You were so sexy in that black cape and, ooh, what a charmer. I bet you had all the girls on that film. I'd've let you bite my neck anytime.'

107

For a moment there was no reaction, then his eyes flickered and he registered her presence.

'There we are.' She kept her eyes on his all the time, keeping his focus on her. 'Charmed to meet you, Signore Aguletti. Though I had hoped it would be over a bottle of Chianti and a nice parpadelle.'

Panda rolled his eyes at her flirtations in the face of danger. 'Get on with it, woman. Ask him where the demon is.'

At the mention of the demon his eyes fell. *'Piccolo demone,'* he said in a broken monotone. 'It eats...the hearts for me. *Mi dispiace.* So...sorry.'

Iris took his hand. 'I understand. It's feeding on your fear, Signore, that you aren't as great as you were. It's taking the heart from other actors and eating it to give you more heart, more passion, more drive. Everything they had you have now. But, chuck,' she smiled grandly at him, 'you were great. You will always be great. You don't need this little demon.' She paused. 'You know that. Why else would you draw us the pictures to warn us if you weren't horrified at what it had made you do.'

Panda piped up. 'He's not an alien, Iris. So how did he get this demon inside him?'

Iris looked at Magnus, sending the question to him with her gaze.

'Julio,' he said woodenly. 'I saw his...rites.'

'That dratted conceited arse!' cried Iris. 'I said he'd called up something, didn't I, Panda?'

She turned back to Magnus. 'It's OK. We're here to exorcise this demon from you.'

Magnus's expression changed to one of great melancholy. 'It is...hard to...get it...back. It wants...life...outside me. But...I must...get it...back. It gives me...life now. Without it...I am...*niente*...nothing.'

'Oh chuck,' said Iris sadly. 'You have to believe in yourself. You're one of the greats! An Orson Welles, a Cary Grant, Richard Burton, James Stewart...'

'Iris,' hissed Panda, 'They're all American!'

'Er,' she continued stumblingly, 'Mastroianni, Benigni, ah...Lugosi?' She shook her head. 'Never mind, chuck. Everything will be fine. Just you leave it to Signora Magnifique and her trusty Panda. Now, where's this demon?'

Suddenly his eyes flickered. But not to look at her. Looking at something beyond her. Shivers went down her back.

'Iris…' said Panda, anxiously.

She turned, slowly.

On the floor behind her was the demon. It was a pink lump of scarred tissue the size of a baby with a hideous face – cruel red eyes, vicious teeth; tiny stumpy arms reached out for her with small but wicked claws. It threw itself at her, scrabbling at her chest.

Iris gave a girly cry and pitched over onto the floor. Red eyes full of hate glared into hers. A terrible wet gurgling came from its mouth. She had her hands around the repulsive slippery body, trying to rip it from her but its grip was too strong. She imagined those hands could easily punch through her chest and fix around her heart.

Abruptly light flashed into her eyes, stunning her. The pop of a flash going off, again and again. The demon squealed and was suddenly gone from her chest. Panda was at her face, gently pawing her back to awareness. She waved him away, noticing the camera by his side.

'Where's it gone?' she said, standing too quickly, wobbling on her feet. Then she saw Magnus on the lounge, struggling with the demon, shoving it back inside his body. The little creature was screeching, scratching frenziedly at him. Vicious red cuts appeared on his face and his hands. But Magnus held his demon, pushing it back into the tear in his chest.

'No, Magnus,' cried Iris. 'You can't control it! You must let it out.'

Magnus ignored her. He picked up a spray can that lay at his feet and began to spray the tear in his chest. A clay-like substance covered his skin, and immediately began to harden, sealing the demon inside.

'Aha,' said Panda, 'I knew it. Production trickery.'

Iris was fuming. 'Magnus! Stop this at once!' Showing no sign of listening to her, she tore across the room at him.

Magnus, seeing her coming, raced from the room, still trying to hold the demon in his chest.

Pausing only to pick up Panda, Iris raced after him.

They chased Magnus through the peeling, darkened mansion corridors until they arrived at the main set. The red swans leered suggestively at them. The set was silent, lit only by a single light from the lighting gallery. Iris peered around the room with a hawk's gaze.

The pool of light shifted slightly. Iris looked up. A shadow flitted across the lighting gantry.

'Up there, Panda!' she said.

'I don't like heights,' he replied grumpily.

There was a crash as a light smashed to the floor centimetres from them.

'Up, up, woman! Stop dillydalling and get up there.'

Iris, an accomplished climber, shimmied up the ladder quickly.

The lighting gantry was dark. Iris peered over the railings to the set below. It appeared a long way down. She slowly and carefully tip-toed over the grating, her eyes peeled for any movement in the darkness.

'Magnus,' she cried, and her voice echoed eerily in the shallow space, 'we are here to help you. That demon does not belong in you. You can't keep it.' She paused, listening, waiting. Nothing. 'Let us help you.'

'I can't see a thing,' complained Panda.

'Hang on, chuck, I have a torch here somewhe -. Ah. '

The instant she flicked on her pencil torch, it illuminated Magnus reaching out for her with a maniacal expression. There was a moment of startled shock, then her instincts kicked in. She ducked, turning her momentum into an upward strike. Her head hit Magnus in the chest, his most vulnerable area. With a surprised cry, he fell over the railing backward. There was a judder as the lighting scaffold was subjected to a weight.

Taking a deep breath Iris looked over the side. Magnus was hanging there.

'Hold on, chuck!' Iris pulled out a dirty handkerchief and, with some objection, knotted it around Panda's paw.

'I think I'm going to be sick,' he said as she lowered him over the railing.

But her improvised Panda-lifeline did not quite reach.

'Come on Magnus. Reach up. We'll get you out of this.'

Magnus was terrified, his eyes bulging. Tentatively, he unclasped one hand from the gantry and reached up. His fingers brushed Panda.

'For god's sake, you pathetic B-grade,' Panda snapped. 'Do you think I like hanging about in mid-air? Stop waving your hand and do something with it!'

Galvanised by Panda's directorial tone Magnus stretched and took hold of a furred foot, pulling Panda down with an aggrieved 'Oof'.

But then there was a terrible crack.

They all saw Magnus's chest bulge open. A tiny clawed hand pushed its way out. Magnus locked gazes with Iris, clearly in pain, and she knew with certainty that he couldn't let the demon go. There was a cinematic pause. Another terrible crack. And Magnus let go, wrapping his arms around his chest, keeping his precious new life, his *piccolo demone* inside. As he fell he twisted and landed with a loud thud head first on the set. A pool of red slowly began to leak from his smashed body. A tiny claw under him twitched once and then lay still. The red swans looked with blank uncaring stares at this dramatic final scene of the drama.

Iris sat down hard on the lighting gantry. Panda came up to her. 'I thought if we could just save one of them...'

Panda cocked his head at her hypocrisy but his reply was kind, 'You said we couldn't. This is history. It's taken its course.'

As though he had said something alarming, Iris blinked and got to her feet. 'Yes, we should be getting on. Remind me to pick up that camera on the way. Keep our piccies out of the police report this time.'

'Isn't that tampering?' asked Panda.

'If there is one thing this little adventure has taught me, my dear Panda, it's that you should always do what you're best at.'

Back in the bus, sipping on a gin and tonic, Panda was beginning to feel almost his old self.

'Not sure I can handle another one of those,' he said to Iris as she got behind the wheel.

'Yes, we'll try for something lighter next time. A comedy perhaps?' She was downcast for a moment. 'Still, what a pity that I didn't get my fifteen seconds on the big screen.'

'Thousands of sighs of relief are heard all around the world,' Panda replied. Iris was about to retort angrily when he continued. 'Besides, you're much too good to be known for a B-grade horror role in a film no one was ever going to watch.'

Iris grinned at him. 'Oh, my little film critic, you'll be surprised then when I tell you *La Danza Rosso* has a cult following?'

'What? How can it possibly?'

'Well, all ten minutes saved from the fire, that is.'

'Fire? What fire?' He was suddenly suspicious at her knowing tone.

'Didn't I tell you, chuck? The whole mansion burned down mysteriously in a great fire. The police spent months piecing together what happened.'

'Iris? Look at me.' This is it, he thought. If she had anything to do with this fire he was getting off at the next stop.

'What lovey?' She looked at him with utter guilelessness. She had already forgotten all the deaths and was thinking about the next adventure.

He sighed, sipped his gin, decided to drop it. He said, 'How about some music? And then you can take us somewhere without a single actor in sight.'

Iris turned back to the wheel and scrabbled about in her cassettes. 'Excellent idea, chuck. Ooh, what about some Bowie. He always cheers me up.' She selected a tape and pushed it into the player. 'And I know just the song, too.'